ALLISON AND THE BIG APPLE

Letitia led me through the back door into the house. The halls and rooms were all painted a pale tan, and the furniture looked a lot like the stuff we have back in our junior high school lounge. And the walls were hung with children's drawings, which all looked like your standard little kid scrawls—except for one.

It was a portrait of Letitia—except it wasn't a traditional portrait. The colors were all wrong, the proportions exaggerated, and yet, it was more *her* than any realistic painting or photograph could have been.

"Wow," I said. "This is great. Who painted this?"

"A friend," Letitia said quickly.

I squinted and looked closely. There was an initial scrawled at the bottom right corner. *M.* I had a sudden hunch.

"The mysterious Malcolm?" I asked.

Letitia nodded. "That's right. Now about the computer . . ."

"He's really talented. Where is he that he's not coming back?"

Letitia sighed heavily. "Can we not talk about that right now? Please?" There was real pain in her voice, and in her expression. For the first time this whole visit, she looked like the cousin I remembered from that long-ago summer in Mississippi.

I nodded. If she didn't want to talk now, th[...] all right with me. "Sure," I said, sitting dow[...] of the computer. "Let's see what you have[...]

Look for these other exciting *Adventurers, Inc.* titles!

Ready, Set, GO!
Susette's Awesome Adventure
Rosina Saves the Day

Adventurers, Inc.

#4:
Allison and
the Big Apple

Mallory Tarcher

Z·FAVE
KENSINGTON PUBLISHING CORP.

Z*FAVE BOOKS are published by

Kensington Publishing Corp.
850 Third Avenue
New York, NY 10022

Z*FAVE is a trademark of Kensington Publishing Corp. The Z*FAVE logo Reg. U.S. Pat. & TM Off.

First Printing: November, 1994

Printed in the United States of America

This book is dedicated to:

Dave—my love, my friend, my family

*And to all the horses at Claremont Riding Academy,
New York City*

The only way to have a friend is to be one.
—Ralph Waldo Emerson

One

Dear Mom,

From the wilds of Maine to the lights of the big Apple—I bet this is going to be the biggest contrast of our trip. And I have to admit, I'm ready to give all the nature a break. No mountains, no rivers, and no deserted islands. Just shopping, shopping, and more shopping. Oh, no! I think spending all this time with Rosina is starting to affect me. What I *mean* to say is that I'm really not going to get into any trouble on this trip. None. Zero. Zip. I'm turning over a new leaf.

Honestly, Mom, this trip is so great. I've never met so many different people or had so many exciting adventures in Santa Barbara. Anyway, New York City, look out! The Adventurers are about to hit town. I'll give your regards to Broadway and I promise I'll be careful.

Love, Toni

Dear Mama and Papa,

Civilization at last. Even though I found Maine more—well—exciting than I thought I would, I still can't wait for a decent hotel, some fabulous shopping and a more sophisticated atmosphere.

Did Fuzzbrain arrive safely? I think about him all the time. Remember to feed him lots of treats—okay?

John hasn't said where we're staying. I hope it's the Plaza. Do you remember when we went to New York for Christmas that year, Papa? I'll never forget ice skating in Central Park. I hope the summertime in New York is as exciting as the winter. I'll let you know in my next letter.

With love, Rosina

Dear Mother and Father,

We are traveling by train from Boston to New York. John drove us from Maine in a minivan and I got to see a lot of the scenery. I really like traveling by train. Somehow it feels so safe and predictable. Sailing in Maine was quite interesting once the seasickness went away. I'm really beginning to get to know the other girls and am starting to feel like we are all becoming very good friends. Please tell Grandfather I will write the next letter to him.

Love, Susette

Dear Mom,

First of all, you probably want to know about Maine. For a change, Toni wasn't the one who got us into trouble. It was Rosina—but surprisingly, she helped get us *out* of trouble, too. I guess you never can tell about people.

But you know, as much fun as I'm having on this trip so far, I actually miss all the boys—don't tell them I said that! It sure will be good to have family around for a while. Can you believe that I'll finally get a chance to see Aunt Sara and cousin Letitia? How long has it been? Six years, I think. The fact that I get to see them in New York City is even better. Do you think they'll recognize me right away? I was only eight when Letitia and I spent that summer at Granddad's farm. I wonder how Letitia likes living in Brooklyn. I remember how much she liked Mississippi—I can't picture her as a city girl.

I'll give them both your love. I bet they haven't changed a bit.

Love you, Allison

I shook my head at the shaky writing on the outside of the envelope as I folded the letter to my mom and put it in my backpack to mail when we got to New York. The train lurched around another corner and a suitcase came flying off the overhead rack. It hit the floor right behind me and popped open. I didn't even have to look around to know who was scrambling frantically to scoop up the piles of clothing. Only a suitcase that was packed too full would pop open like that.

Rosina Iglesias was muttering about so-called modern transportation in the twentieth century as she knelt on the floor of the swaying train. I eased out of my seat and started grabbing handfuls of silk blouses as I shot her a sympathetic glance. Rosina's long, light-brown hair was pulled back in a perfect ponytail and her bright blue T-shirt looked like it had just been unfolded from a pile at the Gap. Rosina would look pulled together in a tornado, I thought, although after watching her stuff her clothes back into the suitcase and sit on the lid to close it, I didn't have any idea how she pulled it off.

In fact, the first time I met her, I never thought she'd make it on this trip without taking along a personal servant or two. She's kind of spoiled, being an only child. Did I mention, an only child of very wealthy parents?

I'm used to doing things for myself whenever I can. Not that I get the chance very often. With five older brothers, I'm lucky to have an unprotected moment. Anyway, I thought Rosina would be totally useless, but I was wrong. She's not at all like I thought she was. I guess I just needed to give her a chance.

I mean, when we were in Maine, she lost her favorite pair of earrings, really expensive diamond studs. To make up for it, we three bought her a pair of cool globe-shaped earrings. We bought a pair for each of us, in fact—you know, for the Adventurers. As soon as Rosina told her parents she'd lost the diamonds, they sent her a new pair, even more sparkly than the first. But do you know that Rosina hasn't worn them yet? She's still wearing the cheap—and kind of goofy—earrings we bought her. Neat, huh?

As I stood up to help Rosina shove her suitcase back on the overhead rack, I could see Susette Yoshi stretched out across two seats ahead of me. She was writing intently in the journal she is keeping about this trip. Susette told me she wants to be a writer, and ever since then I've had the idea that although she doesn't always say very much, she always knows exactly what's going on.

Susette is from a really strict Japanese-American family, and when I first met her I got the impression that she was strictly a speak-to-when-spoken-to type of person. Slowly but surely, though, she's been loosening up. One of these days I'd love to see her really break out and do something unexpected.

Susette's really pretty. Small, with beautiful dark hair and a perfect complexion. But I think she tries to make herself look really plain. You know, no makeup, straight hair parted in the middle, always wearing jeans and a blouse. She'd be so great-looking with one of those really short haircuts all the magazines are showing for spring, and maybe some red lipstick—but trying to get her to change her look has been nearly impossible so far. Except that one night when she kissed Tommy Tilousi back when we were at the Grand Canyon. But you know that story already.

Susette and Toni Francis are total opposites in the sense of doing unexpected things. Toni is my best friend ever. And she'll try *anything* once. Heck, I never even have to suggest it. And half the times I have, I wish I hadn't. I looked across the aisle to where Toni was curled up in her seat, fast asleep. Her long, curly brown hair, which, much to her dismay, usually has a life of its own, was tucked up under her San Francisco Giants baseball cap. But even sound asleep, I could see a shadow of her typical grin creep across her face.

I knew that if she were awake, her green eyes would be sparkling with excitement as she described her latest plan for adventure. My brothers—all five of them—love Toni. She's so tiny and pretty and they're all big, hulking beasts. Generally they laugh at all her antics, which of course makes her furious. I've grown used to it—being laughed at, I mean. Where Toni fights to show them she can do things, I guess I've gotten used to letting them take over when they insist. See, the truth is, I know I can do almost anything they can do, and even some things that they *can't.*

My name is Allison Morris. People tell me I look kind of like Janet Jackson, except for my brothers, who tell me I look fat. But what are brothers for if not to keep your ego in check?

And what was I doing, sitting on a Boston to New York Amtrak train with four other junior-high girls from Santa Barbara, California? Broadening my horizons, of course. Seriously. The Santa Barbara's Women's Council sponsored an essay contest last spring. The winners of the contest won a trip around the world for the summer. Toni, Susette, Rosina, and I are the winners.

Of course, it's not like the Santa Barbara's Women's Council is about to just give four fourteen-year-olds plane tickets and wave good-bye. Although, based on what has happened so far in this trip, they might as well have! Nevertheless, trying his best to keep us all together is Mr. McGonigle—who we all call John—once a high-school history teacher, now a bodyguard, chaperone, and tour guide who is bound to have a few gray hairs in his curly black hair by the time he gets us all home again.

Helping out John is Toni's sister Debbie Francis. She's eighteen, tall, blondish, and *totally* in love with John. Because of this, I'm sure she thought this would be *the* dream summer job. Boy, was *she* in for a surprise! Still, even though she and Toni fight like cats and dogs, there are moments between them that make me wish *I* had a big sister to talk to.

So far, we've been to Vancouver, British Columbia; the Grand Canyon; and Maine. Pretty much the more rugged areas of the North American continent. But now we were just minutes away from New York City. I was looking forward to the skyscrapers and concrete—civilization at last! At least there'd be no disasters in a mine shaft, no near drowning in a raging river, and no sailing through thunderstorms. Instead, we'd visit museums, take in a few Broadway shows, go shopping, and maybe even see a few celebrities!

But best of all, at least from my perspective, I'd have

a chance to introduce everyone, especially Toni, to my favorite, coolest cousin. You know how excited you get when you know two of your favorite people are going to hit it off? That's the main reason I was so excited about seeing Letitia and Aunt Sara.

At the beginning of our trip John had told us that if we had any relatives in any of the places we'd be visiting, we should tell him so we could plan to see them. He said it would give us a better idea of how people actually *lived* in places where we would otherwise just be tourists. I really liked the idea of seeing what it would be like to live in New York, so I wrote to Aunt Sara and told her we were coming. I was thrilled when Aunt Sara wrote back and told me that she and my cousin Letitia would pick us up at Penn Station.

"Allison, do you think you'll recognize your cousin?" Susette had put her notebook away and moved back a few seats. Being careful not to wake up Toni, she slid into the seat across the aisle.

"I think so," I said. "Since I was eight years old, I've kept a picture of the two of us, sitting bareback on one of my granddad's retired farm horses. It's a goofy picture. We've both got these really dorky braids that stick out on either sides of our head, and we're dressed exactly alike in overalls and checked shirts. We dressed the same all that summer." Even though I hadn't seen Letitia in about six years, I still remembered her pretty well.

Susette smiled. "Sounds like she's the sister you never had."

"Who wants a sister?" Toni struggled to an upright position, scrubbing a hand across her eyes and yawning hugely. "I've got one you're welcome to."

"Allison was just talking about her cousin—the one that we're meeting at the train station," Susette explained.

"Oh yeah—Letitia. Right, Ally-Cat?" Toni was wide awake in a second. There never seemed to be any transition between her being awake and being asleep. "I can't wait to meet her. If she's half as much fun as you, this will be the best part of our trip so far."

"New York's going to be the best part anyway," Rosina said, joining the conversation. "Until we get to Paris, that is."

Rosina's like that. She can stop a conversation cold, by just implying that she's already done the very thing you're talking about getting ready to do.

"You've been to New York before, right, Rosina?" I jumped in before Toni could make some kind of a sarcastic comment. The hardest thing about traveling with Toni and Rosina is that they both think they know it all. The only difference is that one is sarcastic about it and one is snobby about it. Sometimes I feel like a referee, and I guess Susette does, too, because at that moment I saw her glance at me gratefully.

"I go about twice a year with my parents," Rosina

said. "Usually to get some new clothes. The stores in New York are some of the best in the world."

"Nothing like the ones in Paris, though," Toni added knowingly.

"Oh, which store in Paris is your favorite?" Rosina asked sweetly, knowing she had Toni on that one. We *all* knew Toni had never been to Paris.

"I like *Alors.*" Toni smiled. "The clothes are *so* funky there!"

Rosina raised an eyebrow. "That's one of *my* favorites, too. Do you *really* know it?"

"Of course," Toni replied innocently.

The three of us stared at her. How could we argue? We knew Toni had never been to Paris; she'd pulled the name of this store out of the air. This round goes to Toni, I thought.

"Next stop, New York, Penn Station." The conductor made his way down the length of the car, using the backs of the seats to keep his balance as the train swayed. "Five minutes to New York, ladies."

We all jumped up and began pulling our luggage down from the overhead racks. Toni came over beside me and stood up on a seat to reach her suitcase. She gestured at Rosina.

"I can't stand it when she acts like such a know-it-all," she muttered.

"How did you know about that store?" I whispered. "You've never been to Paris."

Toni giggled under her breath. "I totally made that

up. It was the only French word I could think of. I just can't *believe* she fell for it."

I shook my head as I tossed my nylon travel bag onto the seat and turned around to reach for my other bag across the aisle. As I hauled my big suitcase down, Rosina reached up to give me a hand.

"I hate it when Toni won't admit she doesn't know something," Rosina said under her breath. *"Alors.* Really. There's no such store in Paris."

She started to laugh, and I couldn't help myself. I cracked up too. There's nothing like two stubborn people to make a situation look totally ridiculous.

"What's so funny, Ally?" Toni was lugging her bags down the aisle toward the exit, her head turned over her shoulder, looking back at me, expecting an answer. She didn't even see John until she bumped right into him. I breathed a sigh of relief that I wasn't going to have to explain my laughter to her.

"Okay gang, here we are." John raised his voice a little so we could all hear. "I'm sure I don't have to remind you—"

"But you're going to anyway," Toni muttered, getting herself a quick elbow in the ribs from Debbie, who had materialized at John's side.

"—that New York City is not Santa Barbara—or Maine, for that matter." John was getting pretty good at ignoring Toni when it suited him.

"Therefore," he continued with a grin, "I don't expect that any of you will be falling into an old mine, or rafting down a violent river—and *I* promise not to lie helplessly on a beach with a raging fever." We all exchanged looks. Yep, it sounded like New York was going to be pretty calm after our recent trips.

"I do, however, expect you to follow a few basic safety rules," John said, his voice serious. "If you're carrying a purse or shoulder bag, wear it with the strap across your body like this." He borrowed Debbie's bag to demonstrate.

I could hear Toni start to snicker, and realized that we were all about to lose it at the sight of a *male* teacher wearing a girl's purse slung across his chest.

I think John realized it too, because he turned a little red and started talking more rapidly.

"If you're wearing a backpack, keep it buckled. Don't stop to talk to strangers on the street and try not to stare at anyone, even if you think they're acting strangely. And above all, *stick together.*"

He stared at Toni. "This is the one city on our trip where I can actually imagine losing one of you—and not being able to find you, ever."

Toni shifted uncomfortably. She seemed on the verge of saying something, but then simply nodded.

John nodded too. He seemed satisfied with his speech.

As soon as he turned around, we broke into our usual excited chatter. As we filed off the train, I could see John shaking his head as Debbie patted his arm.

Two

Somehow I got stuck behind Rosina as she struggled with the wheels on her huge suitcase. So far, Rosina's luggage had caused more delays than the weather. Usually I'm pretty patient, and a lot of times I even help her with her bags—but this time, I just wished she'd hurry. Letitia and Aunt Sara were waiting! Our trip to New York wouldn't really start until we met up with them.

The trains that run into Pennsylvania Station in New York City arrive about two levels underground. We had to travel up one of the longest escalators I'd ever seen just to get to the first level.

"Where's the waiting room?" I'd managed to get past Rosina and her huge suitcase and up to where John and Debbie were waiting for us to catch up.

"It's one more level up," John said, pointing at a sign that hung just ahead of us, right above another escalator.

"Why don't the trains just come into the station at street level, like everywhere else in the world?" Debbie grumbled.

"There's not enough room in New York to build a station above ground." Rosina had caught up to us, her suitcase rumbling along beside her. She obviously had decided to play tour guide.

"And if you think *this* is bad, wait until you see the subway. It's crowded, noisy, dirty, smelly . . ." She shuddered. "We should take cabs everywhere."

We all fell silent as we arrived at the top of the last staircase and looked out into the main waiting area of the station. Crowds of people rushed back and forth. Dozens of small stores that looked exactly alike sold everything from food to cosmetics to magazines and clothing.

"Whoa, you could *live* in here." Toni stood open-mouthed, watching the hustle and bustle.

"I think some people do." Susette gestured with her head toward a group of people underneath one of the escalators. They were folding up dirty old blankets and pushing aside cardboard cartons under the watchful gaze of a policeman.

"It's just like Los Angeles, I'll bet. Homelessness is a real problem in New York," John explained. "There just aren't enough systems and services to help everyone who needs help. And then there are those people who just fall through the cracks."

We all fell silent for a moment. I knew everyone was thinking about how lucky we were to have homes and families.

"Well, let's not just stand here and gawk like tourists," Toni said, breaking the silence. "Let's go find Allison's aunt and cousin."

She grabbed my arm and dragged me into the crowd.

Now, I'm sure I've mentioned how tiny Toni is. Well, in the crowd jammed into Penn Station, I felt like we might as well have been invisible.

I glanced behind me as Toni plowed through the masses like she'd been living in New York her entire life. I caught an occasional glimpse of one of the others as we dodged and wove through the other travelers.

"Well? Do you see them anywhere?" Toni paused in a clearing in the middle of what must have been the waiting area. There were about a hundred dirty plastic seats bolted to the floor, and a big information booth in the center.

As I was scanning the area, John and the others arrived.

"You navigated that crowd like a native," Rosina told Toni admiringly.

"Yeah," Toni nodded. "I kind of feel like I belong here."

I could hear a low moan from John as he processed what that could lead to.

I continued to look around. I tried to imagine what Letitia would look like: tall, thin, about six years older than the last time I'd seen her, and probably very sophisticated. After all, she'd lived in New York her entire life.

"Is that them?" Toni pointed across the room to a well-dressed woman with a girl who looked about our age.

I looked carefully. The girl was tall and thin, dressed in tight-fitting jeans and a really cute little crop top. Her hair was straightened and pulled up in an elaborate twist.

It could have been Letitia, I thought, but the heavy woman with her was *not* my Aunt Sara.

"Nope," I replied.

"That's kind of how I picture your cousin, from hearing you talk about her," Toni said.

"Toni, Allison! C'mon over here!" That was John calling. I could hear his voice, but couldn't see him. Where—

"Allison Morris, you haven't changed a bit, child!" Suddenly a tall woman wearing a floral print dress materialized out of the crowd.

"Aunt Sara!" I flew toward her and into a great big hug. It felt like coming home. Aunt Sara was tall, like my dad and brothers, and had the same wide smile they did.

"Where's Letitia?" I stood on tiptoe to look over her shoulder.

"Don't tell me you don't recognize your favorite cousin!" Aunt Sara stepped aside and I found myself face to face with . . .

A total stranger!

My mind sort of went blank as I stared at the person in front of me. You know what it's like when you're expecting one thing, but get something else entirely? Sometimes it takes a minute for you to figure out what's wrong.

And it's not like anything was wrong—exactly. It's just I had that stupid picture in my mind of us on Granddad's horse and I guess I was expecting Letitia to be wearing braids and overalls. Or still to be eight years old.

But the person in front of me was a total stranger. She was a little shorter than me, and a little heavier. I might have recognized the Letitia I remembered if she hadn't been wearing those small round sunglasses with red lenses. I gave myself a quick mental shake. Okay. So she had dreadlocks instead of pigtails and was wearing real baggy pants slung low on her hips instead of overalls. But she was still my cousin. We were family—right?

"Hey, cousin!" I went to give her a hug, but realized that she was staring at me in just the same way I'd been staring at her.

"Hey, Cousin," Letitia said. "Long time no see."

Long time no see? I stared at her. No hug? No reminiscing? Who *was* this person?

And then I became conscious of everyone else staring at me and Letitia.

"You must be Letitia." Toni stepped between us, her hand outstretched toward my cousin. "Allison talks about you all the time."

I waited for Letitia to say something similar; after all, I'd written her about the trip, and told her a little bit about everyone. I was sure she could guess who Toni was.

Toni stood there smiling, her hand out for Letitia to shake. She's so close to the rest of my family, my parents and brothers, I knew she was thinking she'd fit in with Aunt Sara and Letitia just as easily.

Unfortunately that wasn't the case.

Letitia looked at Toni's outstretched hand and arched an eyebrow. "Nice T-shirt," she said. "Madonna, right?"

"You bet. It's autographed on the bottom here, see? I snuck into her hotel room in L.A. and got her to sign it." Toni was really proud of that shirt. "I like your shirt, too. It's really cool," she said, staring at Malcolm X, who stared right back at her from my cousin's chest.

"Oh, and so is yours," Letitia said to Toni. "Not!" she whispered to my Aunt Sara.

I could tell Toni had overheard Letitia's nasty remark. I struggled to think of something to say to cover up the awkward silence. "Um . . ."

Fortunately, everyone else seemed to have the same idea. They began to introduce themselves at the same time.

"I'm Susette."

"Rosina Iglesias, nice to meet you."

"Hi, I'm Debbie, Toni's sister."

But it was too late. I saw the beginning of a frown between Toni's eyebrows as she pulled at her T-shirt. And I knew just what she was thinking.

She hated my cousin.

Now, Toni's my best friend, but she tends to make snap judgments about people, and I had to let her know that she was just wrong about Letitia. But Aunt Sara was talking to me a mile a minute, asking about my mom and dad and all my brothers. I tried to catch Toni's eye. We're so close that sometimes we can practically read each other's minds. But she had moved over to a newsstand with Rosina and was leafing through a copy of *Sassy*.

"C'mon everyone. Let's get moving." John motioned toward the exit. "They're expecting us at our hotel. You girls can get acquainted on the way there. Sara and Letitia are going to come and help get us settled in."

"Oh, great," Toni grumbled. "Hope I get to sit with her in the cab—not!"

"Hey, Toni." I hung back behind the group and grabbed my best friend by the hand. "Give Letitia a chance, huh? It's probably kind of overwhelming to meet the whole group of us at once."

Toni frowned a minute, then smiled and gave my hand a squeeze. "Sure I will, Ally. You know my motto—any member of your family is a member of my family, too. I could use a new aunt and a cousin."

My spirits picked up. This was going to be all right. It wouldn't take more than a few hours of us all hanging out together before Letitia would be taking us to all the cool places, showing us all the really hip sights in Manhattan. Just like John had said—we wouldn't be just tourists here. We would be doing the things *real* New Yorkers did.

Just then Debbie appeared in front of us. "Let's go, you guys! Everyone's out front, waiting for cabs. John thought he lost you." She stared right at Toni. "And that's not going to happen on this trip. Is it?"

Toni shook her head.

"Good," Debbie said. "Then let's go." Gesturing for us to follow, she turned around and headed off.

Toni made a face at her back.

"Do me a favor, Ally," she said, picking up her suitcase. "The next time I say I want more family members, hit me."

Three

We followed Debbie through a set of swinging glass doors, up yet another escalator, and finally out onto the street. At the curb was a taxi stand, with what seemed like a hundred people gathered around it, yelling and screaming and bumping into each other. A herd of yellow cabs were jumbled together at the curb, so closely packed that I was expecting there to be an accident any second. Car horns were blaring, and as we watched, an ambulance sped up the avenue the wrong way.

Debbie shook her head. "What a madhouse."

I had to agree with her. But Toni spun around on her heels, took it all in, and smiled. "I like it," she said.

Just then John stepped forward. "There you are. I was beginning to worry we'd lost you again," he said, staring directly at Toni.

Oh, no. That was the last thing Toni needed—to get in trouble because I'd asked her to give my cousin a chance.

"It was my fault," I said quickly. "I was window-shopping. Toni stopped to make sure I didn't get lost."

John frowned as if he wasn't sure whether or not to believe me. Toni smiled at me gratefully.

"All right then. But from now on, stick together. I mean it," John added. "You know where we're going, right?" he asked Letitia.

She shot him a dirty look. "I live here—remember? Don't worry about me."

"I'm not worried," John said, though I could tell by the tone of his voice that he was a little annoyed. Great, I thought. My favorite cousin's making a good impression on everybody.

He handed her a twenty-dollar bill. "This is cab fare for you guys," he said, indicating Susette, Toni, Letitia, and me. "We'll see you up at the hotel."

With that, he, Debbie, Rosina, and Aunt Sara piled into one cab. The rest of us got in another.

Somehow, although I was the biggest, I got stuck riding in the middle of the back seat, between Toni and Letitia. Susette was in front.

"It must be pretty cool living here—especially in the summer, when you don't have to go to school," Toni said, leaning across and smiling at Letitia. "I'll bet there are a million things to do."

"Yeah," Letitia said. "If you got a million bucks. Stuff around here costs money."

Toni frowned. "Stuff everywhere costs money—but there are always ways to have fun."

I closed my eyes for a second, wishing that I could start this part of the trip over again. My best friend and my favorite cousin were not getting along at all. And I didn't have the first clue in the world what to do about it.

I sighed and stared out at the scenery that was whizzing past. We were heading up Madison Avenue, one of the most expensive shopping streets in the world. Every store you could imagine lined the sidewalks, and expensively dressed people were strolling along peering in the windows and coming out of the shops loaded down with bags.

I thought about Rosina in the cab ahead of us.

Toni leaned toward me. "Speaking of money—I bet John has his hands full right now," she said, nodding toward the stores on either side of us.

"You read my mind." I laughed. "I bet Rosina's trying to climb out the door at every red light."

Toni leaned back against her seat, smiling.

"So Madison Avenue is your friend Rosina's idea of high culture?" Letitia wasn't amused.

"Well, she *has* managed to do some major damage to her clothing allowance in almost every place we've visited so far," Toni said, still grinning.

Letitia laughed—but it wasn't a nice laugh. "You can take the girl out of Beverly Hills, but you can't take Beverly Hills out of the girl."

Susette hadn't said much the whole ride. Now she turned around in the front seat and spoke directly to Letitia. "Rosina's pretty privileged. I think she sees things a little differently from the rest of us sometimes, but that doesn't mean she's not learning things on this trip, too."

I thought Letitia would have some smart comeback

to that, but to my surprise, she just nodded, as if Susette was right about something. It made me wish that I'd stuck up for Rosina, too.

The cab turned left, onto a block full of small apartment buildings. A couple of blocks ahead of us, I could see a wall of green. Central Park, I realized. Not that we'd be spending a lot of time in a park on this part of our trip. Experiencing New York, I was sure, was not going to involve experiencing the great outdoors.

"Pull over here," Letitia directed the cab driver.

The driver swung over to the curb, right in front of an old, brick-faced building. The awning over the doorway said MADISON ARMS. Letitia paid the driver, and we jumped out and began to lift our luggage out of the trunk.

The other cab pulled up behind us. John climbed out, put his duffel bag on the sidewalk, and started digging in his pocket for some change to pay the driver.

"Hey, you! Come back here with that bag!" Toni yelled at a young man wearing jeans and a black polo shirt. "John! He's got your bag!"

John spun around and in a few long strides had the guy by the arm. He was too far away for us to hear what he was saying, but we could see him laugh and pat the guy on the back.

John turned around and headed back to us—without his duffel bag.

"Quick reaction, Toni," he said when he reached the group. "You just stopped one of the hotel staff from stealing my bag."

Debbie snickered while the rest of us fought like crazy to hold it in.

"You *said* to be careful," Toni protested. Her words were drowned out by a loud laugh from Letitia.

"The country girl in the big city," she joked.

I could see Toni turning redder and redder.

"Hey, it *could* have been something serious," I argued. I felt like I had to defend my friend.

"Well, it wasn't." John gestured at all of us to get moving. "Hey, who got the change from that cab driver?"

"Change?" Susette looked at Toni, who looked at me. I turned to Letitia.

Letitia shrugged. "I told him to keep it. He looked like he needed the money."

"Letitia!" Judging by the look on Aunt Sara's face, she wasn't happy. "That wasn't your money to give away."

Aunt Sara turned to John. "I'm sure Letitia will be happy to make up the difference out of her own pocket," she said.

Letitia reached into the pocket of her jeans and pulled out a crumpled ten-dollar bill.

"This should do it," she said, handing the money to John.

"Next time, maybe you'll give away your own hard-earned money," I overheard Aunt Sara whisper in Letitia's ear as she exchanged a look with John.

I knew what that look meant; I'd seen it too many

times on this trip, mostly when John was trying to get us out of some scrape we'd gotten ourselves into. It was a universally recognized look among adults. Roughly translated, it meant: "Sorry. I don't understand what's going on either."

We went inside the hotel, and after John and Aunt Sara checked us in at the front desk, we crowded into the elevator with our bags and went up to our rooms. As always, Debbie and John each had separate rooms, while the four of us were crowded into one.

And this time, we really *were* crowded. I'd heard space was tight in New York, but I was stunned when I saw what that really meant.

"Bunk beds!" Rosina moaned. "This isn't even a real hotel!"

The room was long and narrow with two sets of bunk beds running head to foot along one wall. There were two bureaus side by side at the far end of the room and a small sitting area with a love seat, a rocking chair, and a coffee table arranged in a little alcove with bay windows.

For one person the room might have been charming. For four people, it was a bit—tight. In fact, it was smaller than my bedroom at home. Still, I had to admire the efficient use of space.

"Tight squeeze," Toni said, throwing her suitcase on one of the top bunks. "I don't think there's going to be room in the closet for all your clothes, Rosina."

"I'll say! This whole *room* is smaller than my closet at home!" Rosina exclaimed in dismay.

Letitia rolled her eyes. "Maybe John can get another room for your suitcase," she said nastily.

At the start of our trip, the rest of us—or at least Toni and me—might have laughed at that remark. But now—especially after what happened in Maine—I knew there was a lot more to Rosina than just a lot of clothes and expensive tastes.

So, instead of laughing, I gave Letitia a dirty look and tossed my suitcase on the other top bunk, right next to Toni. Toni and Susette said nothing.

There was a knock on the door, and Debbie peered in.

"Hmmm, cozy," she said, taking a look around the room. "You lucky girls must have gotten the presidential suite. My room's *much* smaller. And John's is even smaller than that!"

Toni and I exchanged a look. How did Debbie know what John's room looked like?

"John and Aunt Sara are waiting in the lobby," Debbie continued. "We're all going to get some lunch, so meet us down there in five minutes."

Toni gave her a funny look. "John's room is smaller than this?"

Debbie folded her arms across her chest and glared at her sister. "Okay, wiseguy. I saw his room because the desk clerk showed us both and John let me pick which one I wanted."

"Oh, no need to explain to *us,* sis." Toni's voice was as sweet as she could make it. "I'm sure there was a perfectly good reason for you to be in John's room."

I nudged Rosina and smiled knowingly, making sure Debbie could see me. Ever since our trip to the Grand Canyon, where we tried to get Debbie and John romantically involved, we'd been waiting for real fireworks to erupt between the two of them.

"You—I ought to—Five minutes. Don't be late." Debbie stomped down the hallway, muttering to herself.

"Don't tell me blondie has a crush on that wimp of a teacher." Letitia shook her head. "How pathetic."

Wimp of a teacher?

"Can't you find something nice to say about *anyone?* " I blurted, before I could stop myself.

Toni's mouth dropped open in shock. Susette lowered her gaze to the floor. Rosina smiled.

And Letitia just glared at me.

"I'm sorry, Letitia," I began. "I didn't mean—"

"I'll be downstairs." Letitia slammed the door behind her.

I turned around.

"You sure told her," Rosina said. "Good for you."

"I don't want to hear it," I said.

"Why do you care so much?" Toni asked.

I shook my head. Why *did* I care so much? Was it just that I'd been looking forward for so long to showing off my favorite cousin that I was trying to pretend everything was okay. No . . . it was more than that. I didn't know if I could explain, even to Toni.

"Letitia is family," I began.

"Family like *that* you don't need," Rosina snapped.

"What am I supposed to do? Trade her in?" I snapped right back. "It's not like she's a *friend* or something."

Rosina glared at me.

"I believe," Susette said quietly, "that something is bothering your cousin."

I opened my mouth to tell Susette to butt out, too— but then I closed it. What she'd said made a lot of sense. Why else would Letitia be so angry?

"Maybe you're right," I replied.

Once we'd all gotten cleaned up and gone downstairs, I saw Letitia off by herself in the corner of the lobby. Trying not to be obvious, I let Susette, Rosina, and Toni get ahead of me.

"Sorry I snapped at you, cuz," I said, keeping my voice low.

"No harm done," she said.

"Letitia," I said. "Is there something wrong?"

She looked at me strangely for a moment. "Wrong?" she asked finally. "What could be wrong?" And before I could say another word, she walked away, over to where Debbie and John and Aunt Sara were standing.

"We're going to Rumpelmayer's for lunch," John announced.

"It's a New York institution," Debbie added. "At least, according to this friend of mine who used to live here."

"I don't care if it's a cafeteria," Toni declared. "Let's get going. I'm starving."

Once on the street we decided to take a bus straight down along Central Park. Letitia assured us we could walk to Rumpelmayer's from the corner where the bus would drop us.

Aunt Sara fished in her purse and found enough tokens for everyone. We all stood on the sidewalk, and soon a big blue-and-white bus pulled up. We scampered up the steps and, following Letitia's lead, put our tokens in the box next to the driver's seat.

Everyone but Letitia grabbed a seat. Letitia clutched a metal bar overhead for balance. Figuring that New Yorkers didn't think it was cool to *sit* on the bus, I reached overhead and grabbed the bar also.

Out of the corner of my eye, I could see Toni get up, stand on tiptoe, and struggle to keep a grip on the bar. As the bus pulled away from the curb and into traffic, she lost her hold and ended up in a very surprised John's lap.

Letitia laughed out loud and Toni shot first her, then me, a dirty look.

The bus ride was really short, and we were soon at a place where about four streets all intersected and wound around a sort of park in the center. Across the street was one of the fanciest hotels I'd ever seen. As we walked toward it I could see that there were uniformed doormen standing outside and a red carpet that ran from the sidewalk up the steps and into the lobby.

"Bet they have bigger rooms there," Debbie joked.

"That's the Plaza Hotel," Aunt Sara told us. "It's one of the nicest in the city."

"Guess that's practically your home away from home, right Rosina?" Letitia had a way of saying innocent enough things in such a way they sounded somehow wrong—or bad.

Rosina turned red. She had heard the undertone too.

"As a matter of fact, I *have* stayed there a few times," she answered. Her tone was perfectly polite, but she didn't make any effort to continue the conversation. Instead, she turned away from Letitia and said something to Toni.

I felt like crawling into a hole. Somehow, I felt responsible for *everything everyone* was saying—and I just couldn't make everyone get along.

"Here it is." Aunt Sara pointed to a red, white, and blue striped awning. "I've been wanting to come here for the longest time," she said, pushing open the door. "I hear they have the best desserts in the city."

"We must have the same friends," Debbie said, laughing. She and Aunt Sara entered the restaurant together, looked around and smiled at each other.

"It's beautiful," Debbie said. Aunt Sara nodded.

Letitia scanned the room and muttered something. This time, I had to agree with her unspoken sentiment. Everything was beautiful, but a little frilly for my taste, too. There were stuffed animals and lace everywhere. The whole place looked more like a greeting-card store than a restaurant.

But the desserts lived up their reputation. And our simple sandwich-and-soda lunches made even Rosina smile when the immaculately arranged plates were laid out on our table. My tuna-fish sandwich arrived looking more like a work of art than a meal. I was almost torn about eating it—almost. But in the end, hunger won out.

Eating made me feel much better, especially after my slice of chocolate coconut angel-food cake. I wondered if all of us—Letitia included—had just been cross because we were hungry.

"So what are your plans for New York City?" Aunt Sara asked as the waiter cleared away the last of our dishes.

"Today's pretty much mapped out," John answered. "After lunch, a little sightseeing, and then back to the hotel to change for dinner and a Broadway show."

"Very sophisticated," Aunt Sara said, nodding her approval. "What are you going to see?"

"*Cats*. Because it's got the best dancing," Toni said.

Aunt Sara smiled. "And tomorrow?"

"We have to do some shopping," Rosina declared. "And I know where I want to go. The new Barney's. It's practically next door to our hotel."

"What about that Warner Brothers store?" Susette asked. "I've heard really good things about that."

"Shopping." Letitia couldn't have said the word with any more disgust. "I think I'll pass."

"It might be good for you to get out and have some fun, honey," Aunt Sara said.

Letitia shook her head. "I have to be at Restart tomorrow."

"Restart?" Debbie asked.

"It's where I work," Aunt Sara said. "It's a residence for single mothers and their children. We also provide job training and daycare assistance."

"That's terrific," John said.

"In this day and age, it's *necessary*," Aunt Sara replied.

I looked up at Aunt Sara and smiled. I knew something that no one else at the table did—part of the reason she felt something like Restart was necessary. Letitia's dad had walked out on them six years ago and hadn't been back since. She cared about helping single mothers and their children because she knew how hard it was from her own experience.

"Necessary for me, that is," Aunt Sara said. "But Letitia, I wish you would take the chance while Allison is here to spend some time with your cousin."

"I wish I could too, Mom," Letitia said. "But I have responsibilities."

I glanced around the table, sure that Toni, Rosina, and Susette were feeling the exact same way I was. Like a spoiled brat who got to take the whole summer off when there was work to be done.

And the worst thing was, I was sure Letitia said it the way she did deliberately—just to hurt us. To hurt me.

"I know Allison wants to spend time with Letitia too," John said. "So I have an idea. Why don't we all come out to see you at Restart tomorrow night?"

Oh no, John, I thought, glancing across the table at Toni, whose eyes were wide with horror. Please don't do me any favors.

Aunt Sara nodded and smiled. "Come out around seven. We'll give you a quick tour, and then go back to our apartment for dinner."

"Terrific," John said. "We'll spend the day sightseeing like tourists and have a home-cooked dinner like we're residents."

Judging by the look on everyone's face around the table, I knew that at last, Rosina, Toni, Susette, Letitia, and I agreed about something. We all hated the idea.

Four

We finished our meal, and said good-bye to Aunt Sara and Letitia. No one was sorry to see them go—well, Letitia, anyway. I tried to put it out of mind, which really wasn't too hard. New York City is the kind of place where you could get distracted just by standing on the sidewalk and watching all the different people walk by.

"I'm pretty full after that meal." John patted his stomach. "What do you say we walk around a bit—see some sights?"

It was a beautiful day and we all agreed that a walk sounded like the perfect thing.

We strolled into Central Park. I've never been anywhere like it. Growing up in California, where the weather is so nice, I guess I take being outdoors for granted. But in the middle of all the concrete and glass in New York, the green park seemed like a very precious resource.

We walked through the zoo, and stopped to watch the sea lions frolic in their outdoor pool. They were hilarious, diving and knocking each other off the rocks. And the noise they made was incredible. Toni started barking like they did, and I swear the biggest sea lion was answering her back. We were hysterical listening to their "conversation."

We continued down the walkway past the zoo, just taking in all the sights. There were Rollerbladers, joggers, parents with baby strollers, sidewalk artists, guitar players and horses slowly pulling old-fashioned carriages along the roadway.

John consulted the map he was carrying. "It looks like we're right near our hotel," he said.

"And our hotel is right near Madison Avenue," Rosina added. "How about a little *indoor* exercise?"

I groaned. Our first day in the city and already Rosina wanted to drag us into all the shops.

"I'd go look around with you," Susette said.

"Not me." Toni shook her head. "I'd rather hang out here in the park on such a nice day."

To my surprise, Debbie agreed. "I've got a copy of the map, John. I could stay in the park with Toni and Allison, and you could walk over to Madison Avenue with Susette and Rosina."

Toni gave her sister a thumbs-up as John shook his head in resignation.

So we split into two groups, with John taking Rosina and Susette, and the other three of us heading through the park. We agreed to rendezvous back at the hotel later that afternoon.

We had the best time, just hanging out. First there was the game of ultimate Frisbee that Toni got us involved in with these really cool-looking guys who said they were in a band. I thought they seemed more interested in having Debbie play than us, but I wasn't about to tell Toni that. She was so excited! Then we stopped to watch Rollerbladers run slalom races. We stopped at the edge of a huge meadow to get a soda from a guy who had a little cart set up.

Later, I was lying on my back in the grass, staring up at the clouds and thinking how great it was to be hanging around in New York City on a summer day with my best friend and her sister. Debbie was even being really cool. The only thing missing was Letitia. In my picture of this trip I had imagined Letitia hanging out with us and doing things like lying on the grass, staring up at the clouds. Kind of like my sister. Instead, she was a total stranger, who obviously didn't want anything to do with me and my friends.

I sighed and rolled over on to my stomach.

Suddenly Toni jumped to her feet. Debbie sat up so fast her sunglasses fell off. "What's wrong?"

"Be right back." Toni stood up and started running toward the softball fields.

"Where are you going?" Debbie hollered after her, on her feet like she was ready to start running, too.

"I won't even go out of your sight," Toni called out over her shoulder.

Debbie shook her head, but she stayed where she was, hands planted on her hips.

Toni ran across the road and then stopped short. Suddenly we realized what had caught her attention. Coming down a slight hill and around a corner were four people—on horseback.

"Horses!" I couldn't help myself. I was up on my feet and heading toward Toni. I've loved horses ever since I was little. I told you my grandfather kept an old retired plow horse on his farm in Mississippi and ever since I'd met ol' Gumbo, I'd wanted a horse of my own. Of course a horse can't live in the suburbs of Santa Barbara, and as my mother never seemed to get tired of explaining to me, with so many of us in the family, we couldn't have lessons in *everything,* and riding lessons were expensive.

Still, it never hurt to dream, and I dreamed about horses whenever I could. So when I saw the most beautiful horses I'd ever seen right there in New York, I almost couldn't believe my eyes.

I caught up with Toni just as she was crossing back over the road. The people on the horses waved to us before they kicked the horses forward and cantered up the dirt path. It looked like they were just floating out of sight.

"What did they say, Toni—who were they?" Even though I was in pretty good shape, I was panting from my sprint across the meadow.

"You'll never guess!" Toni's eyes had that sparkle that meant she was on to a real adventure.

"We can *rent* those horses!"

"Those very horses? Where?" I couldn't believe it.

"Or horses just like them." Toni was breaking into a run back toward Debbie. "There's a stable on the other side of the park called Claremont. It rents out horses for rides in the park."

"We gotta talk John into taking us over there." I caught up to her in a few long strides. "Whatever it takes—deal?"

Toni grinned at me. That was like our code phrase. It meant one of us wanted something a whole lot.

"Whatever it takes," she promised.

We got back to Debbie, who still hadn't budged.

"Horses." She shook her head. "I don't know why you two are so crazy about those big animals."

"They're beautiful," I protested.

"No—now *that's* beautiful." Debbie pulled her sunglasses down low on her nose and pointed across the field to where a tall blond guy in a baseball cap worn backwards was playing Frisbee with a big Labrador retriever.

"I like dogs, too," Toni said, perfectly aware that the dog was *not* what Debbie was referring to.

"Not the dog, you geek." Debbie tossed her long blond hair and pushed her sunglasses back into place.

"Just wait till you children discover boys. You'll forget about horses soon enough."

Toni and I rolled our eyes at each other. Looked like Debbie was in her woman-of-the-world mode.

"Hey, we better get going," I said, glancing at my watch. "That is, if you don't want to have to explain to John that we were late because you were man-watching."

Debbie blushed. "Why should I care if you tell John I was man-watching?"

"Oh, right." Toni made a face. "Should we tell him you were dog-watching?"

"You can tell him whatever you like," Debbie said, stomping off.

We followed. Of course, we wouldn't say a word to John. Our policy this whole trip had been the same: We wanted our two chaperones to spend as much time together as possible. That way the four of us would be on *our* own more often.

By the time the three of us got back to the hotel, everyone else was showered and getting dressed. Toni and I had to double-time it to catch up, so we never really got to talk about Letitia. And as the night passed, after dinner at a swanky Italian restaurant, going to see *Cats,* and just walking under all the bright lights of Times Square, with more people than I could have imagined crowding next to us on the sidewalks—well, I gradually forgot all about the unpleasant events of the afternoon. And when we finally got back to the hotel, I fell asleep with a little smile on my face.

With or without my cousin, New York was going to be one of the highlights of our trip.

But for some reason, when I woke up the next morning, I wasn't feeling quite so cheerful. I couldn't stop thinking about how badly my favorite cousin had treated all my new friends. So, to take my mind off yesterday, I decided to try and write a letter home. But it was useless. What was I supposed to say about Letitia and Aunt Sara? Would I ever be able to tell Mom the truth? That Letitia was completely different from how I remembered her, that she was completely hostile?

And like Toni had said—why did I care so much?

While I was trying to figure that out, everyone else started waking up.

I decided to worry about my cousin later, and try to have a good time during the day, at least. After we ate breakfast at a coffee shop on the corner (where we had the best bagels I'd ever eaten in all my life!), we took a taxi down Fifth Avenue to the shopping district. It's supposed to be the most famous street in the world for shopping, and I guess it *does* have its attractions. We sure saw a lot of beautiful clothes and beautiful jewelry. And beautiful *people* (most of them dressed in black) trying it all on. And beautiful *salespeople,* who kept wanting us to try the latest makeup, or moisturizing lotion, or some other beauty product that I'd never even heard of.

Don't get me wrong—they do all that sort of thing in the stores out in California, too. It's just that here they seemed so serious about it, like their product was really important. It kind of blew me away.

Everybody else seemed pretty overwhelmed, too. Everyone except Rosina, of course, who kept trying the stuff. She even went up to the makeup counter at one of the stores and was about to get made up before John stopped her.

By the time we reached the public library at Forty-second Street (you know, the library you see in all the movies, the building with the big lions in front of it), I'd had more than enough of shopping. So, it seemed, had the others. We all sat down on the huge stone steps leading up to the library entrance.

All of us, that is, except Susette.

"I'm going to see the library," she said.

"A library?" Toni rolled her eyes. "On summer vacation?"

"This is no ordinary library," John said. "It's really worth taking a look at. Let's get something to eat first, though."

I nodded. "I'm with you on that."

"I'm not hungry," Susette said. "And I'd really like to see the library."

Debbie got to her feet. "I'll go with you," she said.

The two of them disappeared in the crowd of people heading for the library entrance.

"Those look as good to you as they do to me?" John asked, pointing to a nearby hot dog cart.

We all nodded, and followed John.

"San Francisco Giants," the man behind the cart said, nodding toward Toni's baseball cap as he handed her a hot dog.

"That's right," she said. "My favorite team."

The man frowned. "Mine, too," he said. "When they played in New York."

"When they played in New York?" Toni and I looked at each other.

"Sure, right up in the Polo Grounds," he explained. "I saw almost every game when I was your age. Cut school if I had to."

"Cool," I said.

"Walked that little bridge right over the Harlem River when the Giants played the Yankees in the '51 Series. Then they moved to San Francisco." The man shook his head. "Bums."

"Well, *I'm* glad," Toni said. "Otherwise, I'd never get to go see them."

"I'm glad somebody's happy about it," the man answered.

John handed the man the money for the hot dogs. "Bums," the man repeated. He seemed really upset.

In a way, I could understand it. Two of my brothers, Robbie and Kevin, are really big Los Angeles Raider fans. I think they'd *die* if their team moved across the country.

No, they'd probably follow them.

"Can we go see the Polo Grounds? Where the Giants played?" Toni asked John.

John shook his head. "It was torn down a long time ago."

"What about the footbridge? Is that still there?"

"It might be," John said. "But we're not going up to Harlem. It's not a good neighborhood."

As soon as the words were out of John's mouth, I could see he regretted them. Harlem was in the northern part of Manhattan. It has a reputation—probably well-deserved, I guess—as being not very safe. It is also a predominantly black and Hispanic neighborhood.

"I thought we were supposed to have adventures," I argued.

"We are," John said. "Only in New York, our adventures are going to be more cultural."

"*Your* idea of culture," I pointed out.

"It's not that important," Toni said, putting a hand on my arm. "Especially since the stadium's not there anymore."

"Yeah, take it easy," Rosina chimed in. "You sound like Letitia."

I was about to reply when Susette came rushing towards us, Debbie a few steps behind.

"You guys—I cannot *believe* how many books they have in there," Susette said. "And the rooms—they're huge! I could spend the rest of our time in New York in there!"

She was more excited than I'd seen her this entire trip. Well, maybe with the exception of the night she kissed Tommy Tilousi back in Colorado. If loving books had anything to do with it, Susette was definitely going to be a writer.

"Myself, I'm ready for one of those hot dogs," Debbie said.

Susette made a face, and we all laughed.

I had to admit, John was right about the library. We went inside for a few minutes, just to look at the reading rooms. They were enormous. Some of them were even bigger than the houses out in Santa Barbara!

After that, we continued to walk down Fifth Avenue until we got to Thirty-fourth Street, where we stopped to look up at the Empire State Building. We had planned to go up to the observatory at the top, but we all agreed it was too nice a day to wait in such a long line.

Instead, we took a bus down to the South Street Seaport, which is this half mall, half restored-harbor hangout kind of place. There are the usual trendy kind of shops, which, of course, *Rosina* liked, but there are also huge old sailing ships, restored so that you can kind of see what it must have been like to sail the seven seas in long-ago days.

"Those masts must be fifty feet, easy," John said, staring up at one of the ships. "You'd need a pretty big crew to handle a ship that size."

Rosina whistled. "They're beautiful. I wish we could actually go out on one of them."

"Well—why not?" Toni asked. "After our experiences in Maine, I think we could handle it. Don't you?"

Susette, Debbie, and I laughed. And after a second even Rosina joined in.

"I'm ready if you guys are," she said. "I just need to practice coming about again."

"Oh, no," John said, shaking his head. "I think we've had enough sailing for a little while. But there's something else here that should satisfy your curiosity about those ships. Come on."

We followed him down to the next pier, where there was a little movie theater. And what we saw there was a film on the old sailing ships and the entire old South Street Seaport. It was incredible to learn how vital a part of the whole country's economy New York City's piers had been. By the time we left the theater, I had a pretty good understanding of how New York had come to be such an important city.

Our original plan had been to head even further downtown for a ride on the Staten Island Ferry, and maybe even a trip to the Statue of Liberty or Ellis Island. But once we got out of the theater, we realized we were all pretty tired. Plus, it was already four o'clock, so we decided to save those sights for another day, and head back to the hotel to rest before we went to dinner out in Brooklyn.

"I think we got a good start on really seeing New York today," John said.

Rosina, who was walking ahead of us, turned around and frowned. "Don't be ridiculous. We haven't even been to Bloomingdale's yet!"

Five

Rosina and Debbie looked a little nervous. Susette looked scared. Toni looked excited, and John looked like he wanted to hook us all together with handcuffs or something. I was a little nervous myself.

We were about to take our first New York City subway ride.

We had pretty clear directions from Aunt Sara. We were getting on the Lexington Avenue line at Eighty-sixth Street and taking it downtown to Fourteenth Street, where we would transfer to the L train going out to Brooklyn. We'd ride the L for a couple of stops, then transfer to the G train to get to Aunt Sara's.

I had to admit, it was a little scary at first. Especially getting on the train when it pulled into the station. There were so many people, and they were all determined to squeeze on, or off, the train at the same time. As a result, we got a little separated. And the doors shut so quickly! I wasn't sure Toni was going to make it on the car with us.

But once we got going, it was a quick ride. And transferring between trains was much easier than I had thought it would be. But the biggest surprise of all was coming out of the subway into Aunt Sara's neighborhood.

I guess after Letitia's putting down the fact that we came from sunny, perfect Southern California, I'd expected her neighborhood to be pretty run-down. But I thought Fort Greene was the most beautiful neighborhood I'd seen since I'd been to New York City. Big, old, solid-looking houses—with yards, even! The houses reminded me of some of the houses we'd seen in Maine, if you can believe it.

"This is incredible," John said. "I had no idea things were so nice out here."

"There's the house," Debbie said, pointing down the block at a house painted light green. Bushes lined the front yard, and a big sign above the front door said RESTART.

Just as we started walking up the front path, the front door opened and Aunt Sara stepped out.

"Hello, everybody," she said. "I was keeping an eye out for you."

"What a great neighborhood," Debbie said.

"I think so," Aunt Sara said. "I've been here for almost twenty years."

"Where's Letitia?" I asked.

"Out back, with some of the children," Aunt Sara said. "Allison, why don't you go let her know you're here?"

"Sure thing," I said.

"I'll go with you," Toni volunteered.

There was a concrete path leading around the side

of the house. We followed it and found ourselves looking at a big yard, which was almost completely taken up by a children's playground. Three little boys were sitting on the ground. None of them looked happy. With her back to us, facing them, was Letitia.

"I want Malcolm!" one boy yelled.

"Me too!" the other one yelled.

"Well, I miss Malcolm too, honey," Letitia said calmly. "But he's not coming back, and we're just going to have to get used to that."

"He let us play Master Combat all the time!"

"I'd let you play it too," Letitia said. "But the computer's broken right now."

"We want to play Master Combat!"

"Yeah!"

"Let us play!"

Letitia sighed.

"Hello?" I called out.

Letitia turned and caught sight of Toni and me, and managed a wave. She looked exhausted.

"Having problems?" Toni asked. She walked up to the smallest little boy and smiled. "Hey."

He looked up at her. "Gimme your hat."

"Michael!" Letitia shook her head. "That's not how we play here."

"I heard you say something about a computer?" I volunteered.

"You heard *these* guys say something about a computer," she said. "As in, we can't get ours to work, and these guys are going to drive me crazy—aren't you?" she demanded, looking down at the three little boys.

"We want to play!" one said, and a second later, the other two chimed in, and then they were all jumping up and down again.

"What's the matter?" I asked.

Letitia shrugged. "I'm not really sure. We put in a new game card last week, and suddenly the system just started freezing up all the time. We were going to get a serviceman to come by and take a look, but that would cost a hundred dollars." She shook her head. "And we don't have that kind of money right now."

"Hmm. It could be a problem with the interrupts," I said.

Letitia eyed me funny.

"No, really, I know what I'm talking about," I said quickly. "Why don't you show me the computer?"

"Go on," Toni said. "Two of Allison's brothers have computers. She's always tinkering with them. Right, Ally-Cat?"

I nodded.

"Ally-Cat?" Letitia said. "She calls you Ally-Cat? Please." She rolled her eyes.

"Come on, Letitia, maybe she can fix it," one of the little boys said.

"Let her fix it! Let her fix it!" the other two cried.

"I'll take care of these guys," Toni offered. "You go on."

Letitia shrugged. "All right, *Ally-Cat,* we'll give it a go."

She led me through the back door into the house. It was pretty industrial-looking inside. The halls and rooms were all painted a pale tan, and the furniture looked a lot like the stuff we have back in our junior high school lounge. And the walls were hung with children's drawings, which all pretty much looked like your standard little-kid scrawls—except for one I found at the end of the hall.

It was a painted portrait of Letitia—except it wasn't a traditional portrait. The colors were all wrong, the proportions exaggerated, and yet, it was more *her* than any realistic painting or photograph could have been.

"Wow," I said, stopping to study the painting more closely. "This is great. Who painted this?"

"A friend," Letitia said quickly.

I squinted and looked closely. There was an initial scrawled at the bottom right corner. *M.* I had a sudden hunch.

"The mysterious Malcolm?" I asked.

Letitia nodded. "That's right. Now, about the computer . . ." She began to walk toward a room just past the painting.

I followed. "He's really talented. Where is he that he's not coming back?" I asked.

Letitia sighed heavily. "Can we not talk about that right now? Please?" There was real pain in her voice, and in her expression.

For the first time this whole visit, she looked like the cousin I remembered from that long-ago summer in Mississippi.

I nodded. If she didn't want to talk now, that was all right by me. "Sure," I said, sitting down at the desk in front of the computer. "Let's see what you have here."

I turned on the computer and watched it go through its paces.

"It starts out fine," Letitia said. "We can run our accounting program, and our word processing program no problem. But once we try and play games, or use the modem . . ." She shook her head.

"Do you have the manuals for all this stuff?" I asked.

Letitia nodded. "In the cabinet under the desk."

It took me only two minutes of flipping through the manuals to figure out what the problem was.

"I was right—you have an interrupt conflict," I said, turning off the machine.

"A huh?" Letitia asked.

"An interrupt problem," I said. I unhooked the monitor and put it on the floor behind me. "I'm going to open this up, okay?"

Letitia frowned. "Are you sure you know what you're doing?"

"You have a very old modem, and I think it's using the same interrupt as your new game card." I smiled. "What that means in English is that they both have the same address as far as your CPU —central processing unit, which is sort of your computer's brain—is concerned. They're getting each other's mail, and it's locking up your machine."

Letitia shook her head. "You lost me at the modem part," she said. "Go ahead and do whatever it is you have to do."

I took the top of the computer off and changed the settings on the game card. "That should do it. I'll test each of them now to make sure."

I played a couple of different games, both of which worked all right, and then ran her communications program. I dialed up the first number that was listed in her directory and made a connection with the other computer no problem.

"You're logged on," I said cheerfully, watching as the screen changed. It read:

USER: RESTART

WELCOME TO
DSS
Please make your selection from the following menu:
A) Services Directory
B) Procedures & Guidelines
C) News
D) On-line Assistance

"Careful," Letitia said. "Because we get state funds here, we have access to the state government's computer system. Don't go messing around."

"Would I do anything to their machine?" I asked, disconnecting the computer. "After I just fixed yours?"

A smile played around the edges of Letitia's mouth. "My cousin, the computer geek."

"At your service," I said, standing and stretching out a little bit. That's the one thing I hate about working at a computer—your arms and neck get so stiff. And you really have no sense of time passing. Looking at the clock on the office wall, I saw I'd spent a good twenty minutes at work.

But it was time well spent, I decided. Now that I'd proven I wasn't just a spoiled little rich girl from California, maybe Letitia would open up to me.

"So, tell me more about the mysterious Malcolm," I asked casually. "Who is he? Where did he go?"

Her lips tightened, and she shook her head. "Like I said before, I really don't want to talk about that right now."

"Letitia," I said. "I'm your cousin, remember? Not some stranger. Why don't you tell me what's bothering you?"

She was silent a moment. Then she turned away from me and walked across the office to the window. "Malcolm," she said quietly, pressing her forehead to the glass. "I remember coming in to work here one morning last summer, and he was asleep on the office floor. He'd snuck in through this window and just made himself at home."

She unlatched the window, and then turned and looked straight at me. Again, I could see real pain and confusion in her eyes.

"Now I leave it open every night," she said. "Just in case . . ."

Her voice caught in her throat.

"Go on," I said. "You can trust me."

She nodded slowly. "Maybe I can. Maybe—"

"There you are!"

I looked up. Toni was standing at the doorway with the three little boys that she'd volunteered to look after gathered around her. "Sorry to interrupt, but these guys need something to drink, Letitia."

I glared at Toni. She may have been my best friend, but she had a terrible sense of timing. The intimate mood of a minute before was gone.

I decided I was thirsty, too, so we all went to the kitchen. We found everyone else there drinking lemonade and chatting with Aunt Sara about the neighborhood, Restart, and what we had seen, and done that day.

"Well, it sounds like you saw a *lot* of sights today," Aunt Sara said. "So, I'll bet you're all ready for a real home-cooked meal."

"BBQ ribs." John smacked his lips. "I'm *more* than ready."

Aunt Sara smiled. "Best this side of Sylvia's."

"Where's that?" Debbie asked.

"Sylvia's is up in Harlem," Letitia said. "I don't suppose you're going up *there.*" I could almost see the wall Letitia'd begun to drop with me earlier being erected again.

"We were talking about it," I said.

"We were, weren't we?" John added. "I don't know much about that area. What else is up there to see?"

"The Apollo Theater. The Audobon Ballroom—where Malcolm X was shot," Letitia answered, ticking each place off on her fingers.

"And the Jumel Mansion, too," Aunt Sara said. "Don't forget about that."

"Who are the Jumels?" Rosina asked.

"Oh, now, that house has got a history." Aunt Sara smiled. "The oldest house on Manhattan island. Alexander Hamilton built it right after the Revolutionary War."

I shook my head. "Who?"

Aunt Sara frowned. "Don't they teach you *anything* out in California?" She shook her head. "We can continue the history lesson on the way over to the apartment. I've got those ribs marinating right now, and they should be just about ready to stick in the oven. Just let me lock up the office, first. Got to be careful with all that computer equipment lying around."

She pulled out a key ring with about fifty keys on it. "Now where's that key?" she muttered, examining them one by one.

"Here, Mom, use mine." Letitia pulled out a key chain with nearly as many keys, selected a particular key, and handed it to Aunt Sara, who locked the office up tight. Then we set off for their house, Aunt Sara, Toni, and me in the lead, with John, Letitia, Debbie, Rosina, and Susette following.

I don't remember how far we walked. What I *do* remember is Susette and Letitia talking almost nonstop about the Jumel Mansion and its role in American and African-American history. I caught Aunt Sara's eye a couple of times during their talk, and we both smiled. It looked like Letitia really was starting to warm up to us.

Finally, Aunt Sara stopped in front of a big brick apartment building. "Home sweet home," she said.

"Apartment twenty-three, right?" I exclaimed. "I remember writing your address on all those letters, Letitia."

My cousin smiled at that. After that summer at Granddad's, Letitia and I had written to each other pretty regularly for a while. Now, our correspondence had dwindled down to cards at Christmas and birthdays, but I wasn't surprised that I could still recall her address.

Aunt Sara led us into the apartment building. The front door opened into a beautiful lobby, with lots of dark wood and marble floors. Number twenty-three was on the second floor.

"What a great place," Debbie said as we stepped inside.

"Been here almost five years now," Aunt Sara said. "Lot of hard work, getting that woodwork exposed. The people who owned the building before it was converted into apartments really didn't take good care of it."

"Well, *you* have," John said.

"Letitia and I." Aunt Sara looked at her daughter. "Honey, why don't you show the girls your room?"

Letitia nodded, and led us down the hall to a small

bedroom. Well, maybe it wasn't actually small, but it *seemed* that way because it was so packed. Two huge bookshelves overflowed with volumes of every conceivable size and shape. And every square inch of exposed wall was covered with posters and colorful paintings.

"Those prints are beautiful," Toni said, pointing. "They look Haitian."

"They are," Letitia looked surprised. "How did you know that?"

Toni shrugged. "My mom's a travel agent. When my dad was alive, they used to travel all over the world together."

"My great-great-grandparents on my father's side were both from Haiti," Letitia said.

"Really?" I was surprised. "I never knew that."

Letitia nodded. "Sure," she said. "I think I even have a picture of them here somewhere."

"You seem to have a very deep understanding of who you are and where you come from," Susette said. "I admire that."

"I think it's important you don't lose touch with who you are," Letitia said. She walked over to her desk, opened a drawer, and pulled out a photo album.

I stood over her shoulder and watched as she flipped through the album.

"I thought it was in here," she said. "Maybe—oh!" She smiled. "Remember this one, Allison?"

It was the same goofy picture I had of the two of us, from that summer we'd spent in Mississippi. What a geek

I looked like! Big front teeth, stupid little striped top—ew!

"Nice picture, huh?" Letitia asked.

"Please," I said. "Put it away, quickly."

But it made me feel good that she still had it. I started to think that maybe Letitia had pretty good memories of that summer, too.

She flipped the page again—to a picture of a boy a little older than us, with short hair and a pretty cute smile.

"Who's that?" I asked. "He's really cute."

"A friend—nobody important," Letitia said, shutting the album. "I guess that picture's not in here. Sorry." She returned the album to the desk drawer. "I guess you guys probably want to see the rest of the apartment."

I looked at Toni. She just shrugged. Letitia clearly wanted us out of her room, and I didn't know why. Her mood had just changed again. What had we done *this* time, I wondered.

"Come and get it!" Aunt Sara yelled from downstairs. "And you better hurry! The way John's looking at these ribs, they aren't going to last long."

Aunt Sara was kidding, of course. She'd made what looked like enough food to feed a small army. I guess we were a small army, though, because by the time we'd help clear away the dishes, the macaroni and cheese, the collard greens, the biscuits, and all but one rib had disappeared.

"Wow," John said, patting his stomach. "I've never had a better meal."

"And you haven't even had the sweet potato pie yet,"

Aunt Sara said. Just then the phone rang. "Excuse me a minute," Aunt Sara said, and went to the next room to answer it.

When she returned, she looked upset.

"Rachel's in trouble again," Aunt Sara said. "She's dropping off Aisha and Chiffon. They're going to spend the night."

"Rachel," Letitia explained, "is one of the mothers who lives at Restart. Aisha and Chiffon are her daughters."

"Letitia, I'll need your room for the girls," Aunt Sara said.

"No problem, Mom. I'll take the couch." Obviously, Letitia was used to this sort of thing.

"I've got a better idea. That is, if John doesn't mind," Aunt Sara said, glancing at him.

John nodded.

"Why don't you go back to the city tonight with your cousin and her friends?"

Letitia opened her mouth to protest, but Aunt Sara kept right on talking.

"They're going to the Metropolitan Museum of Art tomorrow, and you can show them around." Aunt Sara turned to us. "Letitia's spent an awful lot of time at that museum. She's developed a real interest in art."

"That would be great," John said. "It would save us from having to use a guide at the museum."

Letitia just sat there, her arms folded across her chest. I looked at Toni, who had assumed almost the exact same pose.

"I think it would be great, Letitia," Susette said. "You'd make a *great* guide. What you told me about the Jumel Mansion was really interesting."

My cousin looked like she was softening up a little.

"We don't have enough beds in our room," Rosina blurted.

Letitia turned back into stone.

"Toni's little; she could sleep on the love seat," I replied. I *really* wanted Letitia to spend the night with us. I just knew I could break through to her if we spent the whole day together. And maybe I'd find out more about the mysterious Malcolm.

"I am not . . ." Toni began.

I stared at her. Please, Toni, I thought. Don't make a big deal about this.

She must have read my mind.

". . . too big to fit on the love seat," Toni finished lamely, giving me a look that left me no doubt I owed her one.

I could have sworn that right about then Aunt Sara gave Letitia a good swift kick under the table.

"Fine," Letitia said, with absolutely no enthusiasm. "I'll get my stuff."

"Thank you," Aunt Sara said to John. "I hope you don't mind."

"Not at all," John replied. "It will be good for the girls to spend some time together."

I looked at my friends. I don't think they shared his opinion.

* * *

We made it back to the hotel in what seemed like no time at all.

After calling downstairs for more pillows and blankets, we settled Toni on the love seat, which turned out to be just the right size. Letitia and I each took one of the top bunks.

Everyone was exhausted, and I soon heard Toni's little snoring noises. Rosina had fallen asleep even before we'd turned the lights out, and I suspected that Susette was out cold as well. But for some reason, I just couldn't fall asleep. Usually, I just stretch flat out on my back, close my eyes, and that's it. But I just couldn't get comfortable. I tossed and turned and bunched up all the blankets.

"Letitia," I whispered. "Are you still awake?"

"Yeah." She didn't sound sleepy either.

"Remember when we used to sleep together in the big bed at Grandma's?" I had loved that bed, with its down comforter and piles of pillows.

"Uh-huh."

"We did *everything* together that summer." I smiled to myself, remembering.

"Well, people grow up, Allison," Letitia said. "And they change."

"Family doesn't change," I argued. "And we're still family."

"What does that mean?" Letitia replied angrily.

"Does that mean you come visit me for the first time in eight years and I'm supposed to be your best friend? You don't know *anything* about my life!"

I was stunned by the vehemence with which Letitia spoke. For a moment I didn't know *what* to say. Finally I forced myself to speak. "Well, then tell me about it." I took a deep breath. "Tell me about Malcolm."

"Why? Like I said before, you can't do anything about it. Besides, you're leaving in a week anyway."

"That doesn't mean I can't talk to you," I said. "Family doesn't really go away, ever."

"Oh, yeah? Tell that to my father."

"That was a long time ago," I said lamely. "You've still got your mom."

"That doesn't change anything. I loved my father and he went away." Letitia sounded more sad than angry now. "Just like Malcolm," she added under her breath.

But I had heard her.

"Letitia, who's Malcolm?" I felt like I was on the verge of learning something essential about my cousin, something that I needed to know.

No answer.

"Letitia? Are you awake?"

Still no reply.

I gave up and settled myself on my back. But I still couldn't fall asleep.

And I knew Letitia was still awake, too. Every once in a while I could hear her sniffling quietly in the dark.

Six

I guess one good thing I could say about Letitia is that she doesn't take a lot of time to get ready in the morning. I think it even won her points with Rosina.

She was the first one up and was ready in almost no time at all, wearing what I'd come to think of as her uniform—bright, baggy jeans, an oversized baseball shirt with "Brooklyn" in script across the front, and high-top sneakers.

While we all went through our morning rituals, she sat in the rocking chair, reading one of Susette's books. I thought about what she had said, or rather, about what she had *not* said last night. How could I get Letitia to talk about what was really bothering her, about who this Malcolm was? He *was* important—the kids at the shelter had talked about him, too.

I knocked on the bathroom door.

"I'm almost done," Toni called out.

"It's me, Allison." I didn't want the others to hear me, not just yet. "Let me in for a sec."

I closed the door behind me and quickly told Toni everything Letitia'd said late the night before.

"Her father just left her? He didn't die or anything?" Toni's expression grew serious. Her dad died when she was real little; of all of us, she was the only one who could identify with having just one parent.

"He just took off one summer," I said. "That's why we were in Mississippi. Aunt Sara needed some time to herself. I never knew him at all."

"Is that why Letitia's so moody all the time, you think?" Toni asked.

"I don't know," I said, shaking my head. "Actually, now I think it has more to do with Malcolm than her dad."

"Maybe Malcolm was her boyfriend," Toni mused. "That would explain why she's in a permanently bad mood. She's been dumped. I've seen Debbie act like a crab for *weeks*."

"Hey, are you guys going to hog the bathroom all day?" Rosina pounded on the door. "Susette may be too polite to complain, but I'm not!"

"We know that!" Toni yelled back.

"We'll be right out," I called.

"I think this is the key to understanding Letitia," I whispered to Toni. "I'm going to try to find out who this Malcolm is."

"Well, if he *was* her boyfriend, I can understand why he dumped her," Toni said. "I couldn't put up with her mood swings for too long either."

Just then, the bathroom door swung open. Rosina stood there, glaring at us.

"Hey!" I cried. "Do you mind?"

"Sorry to interrupt, but I heard you talking about foul moods, so I thought I'd share mine with you," she said, her hands on her hips.

"We get the hint," Toni said, brushing past her and out the door. I followed. "The bathroom's yours."

"What was the big conference about, anyway?" Rosina asked before shutting the bathroom door.

Letitia didn't look up from her book.

"Ally, let me borrow your green tank top?" Toni pretended she hadn't heard the question and began to dig through her suitcase, throwing discarded clothing on the floor behind her.

"Don't forget to wear comfortable shoes, Rosina," Susette joked. "You know John said we were going to cover a lot of ground today."

Usually I'm right in the middle of all fashion conversations, but this day, for some reason, I just felt like dressing really plainly.

I pulled on an old pair of jeans and dug around in my bag for any old shirt. I put on a pair of hiking boots and pulled my hair back in a ponytail.

Letitia still hadn't put down her book. *What* could be so interesting, I thought.

Rosina came out of the bathroom and raised an eyebrow. "We are in one of the most sophisticated cities in the world, Allison. You could *maybe* get away with a little more style."

"I just feel like being comfortable today," I said. "If that's all right with you. . . ."

"Breakfast time, girls." Debbie opened the door and stuck her head inside. "Dressing down today, Allison?"

"Is there a dress code I don't know about on this trip?" I snapped.

Debbie's mouth fell open. Even Toni looked shocked.

"Sorry," I mumbled. Gee, I really *am* Letitia's cousin, I thought. Rudeness clearly ran in the family.

We walked down to the corner diner for breakfast. Letitia's mood hadn't just rubbed off on me—it had rubbed off on *everyone*. We had an unusually silent meal—until we were almost finished.

"Ugh," Toni said, pushing her plate away from her. "I think I had too many ribs last night. Who wants to finish my bacon—Ally? Letitia?"

I shook my head. I was having trouble finishing off my French toast.

"I don't eat meat," Letitia replied.

"I noticed that," Susette said. "You didn't have any of the ribs last night."

Why didn't *I* notice that, I wondered, slightly annoyed at myself.

"No meat?" Rosina looked amazed. "How do you do it? And *why?*"

"Meat comes from dead animals," Letitia said. "I don't want an animal to be killed just so I can enjoy a hamburger."

All around the table, everyone had stopped eating.

Debbie pushed the sausage on her plate around with a grim expression.

"My grandfather is a vegetarian, too," Susette said. "I have trouble eating meat myself sometimes."

"If everyone's done, we ought to get going." I noticed that even John hadn't finished his bacon after Letitia's little speech.

"The Metropolitan Museum of Art is huge," Rosina announced. "It could take all day to see it."

"I can't wait to see the Temple of Dendur," Susette said. "I just read that they're allowing people to go inside it now. Imagine being able to walk into a building that's centuries old."

"The *Brooklyn* Museum has the best collection of Egyptian art in the country," Letitia put in. "You'd like it there, Susette."

"Too bad we're not going to the Museum of Natural History today," Toni muttered as she picked up her last slice of bacon and crammed it in her mouth. "I hear they have a *lot* of dead animals there."

I sighed as I got up from the booth. I had a feeling this was going to be a *really* long day.

The Metropolitan Museum was fascinating. There was so much more to see than just paintings. There were entire rooms filled with old furniture and clothing and suits of armor. Toni's favorite were the mummies. Even Letitia seemed to be enjoying herself. She spent a lot of time talking to John, especially when we got to a folk-art exhibit. It seems she had done a lot of reading on African-American folk art, and John talked to her about the exhibit like she was an adult.

But Susette was right. The Temple of Dendur was the highlight of our visit to the museum—in more ways than one.

The Temple isn't just one building—it's an entire complex of them. It's as if the museum people had taken a little piece of an Egyptian village and planted it right in the middle of New York City. Just touching the stone of the buildings gives you a sense of something really old, really mysterious. I actually felt a little tingle run up and down my spine.

"This is *so* cool," Toni said.

I nodded, and stepped back from the Temple itself. The whole display is beautiful. The buildings are on a platform of gray limestone blocks that's set in the center of what is essentially a huge greenhouse. With the sun shining right on us through the tall glass windows, I really felt like I'd stepped backward in time.

"Let's sit down for a second," Toni said.

We sat on a long stone bench, next to Susette and Letitia. They were talking about the designs and images carved on the Egyptian tombs and monuments.

"And the people's features . . ." Letitia was saying. "They were really attractive."

Susette nodded.

"I like *those* features," Toni said, nudging me with

her elbow. She pointed at a boy who was walking around the complex with a sketchpad. He'd look up and study the buildings intently for about thirty seconds, then turn to his pad and quickly sketch something. Then he would repeat the process. All the time, he was walking a path that brought him closer and closer to the bench on we which we were sitting.

"Maybe he'll draw your portrait," I said.

When he reached us, Toni smiled up at him. But he looked right past her, directly at Letitia—and a smile of recognition crossed his face.

"Letitia!" He shut his sketchpad. "I don't believe it. Hey, what's up?"

"Roberto," Letitia said. She wasn't quite as happy to see him as he was to see her. "Long time no see."

"You bet," he replied. "How's things? What's up with Malcolm? Have you heard from him since he went back home?"

She shook her head. "Not a word."

"Oh." Roberto looked surprised. "That's weird. I figured—"

"Look," Letitia said, suddenly in a bad mood all over again. "I haven't heard from him, okay?"

"All right," Roberto said. After a moment he looked at each one of us in turn. "Who are your friends?"

"They're not my friends," Letitia snapped. I saw Susette's face fall. "This is my cousin from California, and these are her traveling companions."

"Pleased to meet you," Roberto said, nodding to each

of us. Then he turned back to Letitia. "You really haven't heard from Malcolm? I wonder what he's doing this summer. I can't believe he couldn't get into the summer program at ArtSpace. He's like—the most talented artist I know."

Letitia shook her head. Clearly, she did *not* want to talk about Malcolm. At least, not with us around.

But *I* wanted to know a lot more about him. So I got up and smiled at Roberto.

"I think he's really talented, too. I saw one of his paintings at Restart. But I don't know anything about him."

Roberto chuckled. "I can't believe Letitia hasn't told you all about the fabulous Malcolm." He didn't seem at all intimidated by the dirty looks Letitia was giving him.

"Hey, there you all are," a voice called.

Oh no, John. What terrible timing.

"Weren't we supposed to rendezvous for lunch at one? It's one thirty now."

Letitia seized the moment. "I'm starving. Let's go."

She grabbed me by the arm and, without even saying good-bye to Roberto, dragged me over to John and Debbie.

"C'mon, let's go eat," Debbie said as we were joined by Rosina, Toni, and Susette.

"Just what we were saying." John shook his head. "I don't know why looking at art gives me such an appetite, but it does."

We left the museum and stood at the top of the wide steps that ran down to Fifth Avenue. It was a gorgeous, sunny day, and suddenly I felt as if I had the whole world at my feet.

"So, where do we eat lunch today?" Debbie glanced up and down the street.

"How about there?" Rosina pointed to a small restaurant across the street.

"That's going to cost a fortune!" Letitia sounded shocked.

"My treat." Rosina had pulled out her AmEx card.

"You have your own credit card?" Letitia's eyes grew wide.

"Never leave home without it," Rosina joked.

Toni and Susette rolled their eyes. They'd heard this routine before, and we knew that in about ten seconds John was going to make Rosina put the card away. But he never got the chance.

"You're all a bunch of spoiled brats!" Letitia exploded. "There are people in this city who don't even have a place to live, who don't even get to *eat* lunch, and who would never in a million years get to travel around the world . . . I bet none of you has ever even *met* a homeless person!" Letitia's eyes glistened with tears.

"Your house looked pretty nice to me," Rosina fired back. "And aside from giving away John's money to the cab driver, I haven't exactly seen *you* trying to change the world."

I was speechless. I looked from Toni, to Susette, to Debbie, to John. I had to fix this—fast.

"Letitia, you're right. We *are* very lucky. And maybe we *are* a little spoiled."

Rosina opened her mouth, and I just glared at her until she shut it again.

"But we don't need any special treatment. Why don't *you* pick a place where we can have lunch like any New Yorker would?"

I held my breath, hoping my friends would back me up.

"That's a great idea." It was John who spoke first. "Letitia, why don't you lead the way."

My cousin set her jaw and stalked down the steps.

We followed her as she stormed up the avenue for about ten blocks and then turned right. We found ourselves in front of a small, run-down storefront. Rosina made a face.

"This is called a *bodega*." Letitia gestured at the doorway. "Not fancy, but plenty of people get their lunch at places like this and eat outside on good days."

We followed her into the store.

"Hola, chica, cómo estás?" The man behind the counter smiled at Letitia. "The usual, sweetheart?"

"Not today, Luis—just a bagel with cream cheese for me—and whatever my friends here want."

We stared at each other. How did this guy know Letitia?

But no one was brave enough to ask. Instead, we all very meekly ordered sandwiches and got cold sodas from the cooler in the back of the store. Then we followed Letitia back out to the street and into the park.

We sat down on benches and began to eat silently. Until Rosina screamed.

"Gross, ugh!" She threw her sandwich on the grass and jumped up, her hand over her mouth.

"Rosina, what's wrong?" Susette was at her side.

Practically crying, Rosina pointed at the half-eaten sandwich.

"There's mold on my bread," she cried. "Give me some soda."

Letitia just sat there, calmly eating her bagel and cream cheese.

Everyone else examined their food very thoroughly. Rosina and Susette sat down again.

"Penicillin is made from mold," Letitia muttered.

John leapt to his feet.

"Okay, that's it. I can't take it anymore. The five of you are behaving like children. One more smart comment, one more mean remark, and you're *all* going to spend the rest of the visit sitting in your room." He stared at Letitia. "And I can arrange that *you* suffer the same punishment."

John had never lost his temper like this before. Not when Toni almost got us arrested at customs, not when Rosina practically killed us in a storm at sea. No, it took *my* favorite cousin to make John threaten to cancel the trip.

I wanted to cry.

My appetite was totally gone. I carefully rewrapped my sandwich in its bag, as if by doing everything very slowly and deliberately, I could keep back the tears already stinging my eyes.

Suddenly I felt a poke in my ribs.

Toni pointed toward the edge of the meadow where we were sitting.

"Look, you guys!" she cried out, breaking the heavy silence. "Horses!"

Seven

Everyone looked at once, grateful for the diversion.
"They *are* beautiful," Debbie said.
"That gray looks like the horse I ride back home."
Rosina sounded wistful. "I wonder where they're
from."
Toni and I shared a look.
"We know!" we said in unison.
We told the others about the people Toni had met in
the park the other day, and about Claremont Riding
Academy. Rosina loved horses; she took lessons
through the year. Susette loved *all* animals. And Letitia,
to my surprise, had been to Claremont before. She told
us that the stable was one of the original riding places
in New York City, and over a hundred years old.
John was happy to see us all agreeing on something.
So in less time than it took to say giddy-up, we had
convinced him to take us for a look at the stable, which
was over on Eighty-ninth Street and Amsterdam Avenue.
Letitia led the way to what we learned was the West
Side of Central Park. As we walked past a huge reser-

voir surrounded by a chain-link fence, she explained that we were walking on the bridle path for the horses. On a level above us, joggers, walkers, and sightseers strolled along a gravel path right next to the fence that surrounded the water.

Along the way she seemed to relax, and pointed out things about the park. "See up in that tree over there? That's an owl's nest. Lots of animals live here in the park. In the mere—up at the north end of the park— there are a pair of falcons. I've seen rabbits and raccoons, too."

We took turns sneaking looks at each other. Was she just trying to make up for what happened at lunch? Suddenly she was like an entirely different person. I remembered how happy she'd seemed that summer in Mississippi. Maybe, despite her tough attitude and urban talk, she was really a country girl at heart.

I felt a wave of sympathy for my cousin. Unfortunately, the connection didn't last long.

We turned to walk out of the park at Ninetieth Street.

"Ninetieth Street? I guess we're uptown pretty far?" I'd hoped I'd asked the question the right way. I'd sort of figured out that the higher the street numbers went, the farther north you were going. And New Yorkers said downtown for south and uptown for north. By my calculations we were pretty near Harlem.

But Toni beat me to it.

"Is this Harlem?" Toni asked, looking at the handsome apartment buildings lining the avenue.

Letitia looked disgusted. "You've got a way to go before you get there," she said in a way that implied she didn't just mean that Toni had a way to go in *miles*.

Toni frowned but didn't say a word.

In about five minutes we had arrived at Columbus Avenue and Eighty-ninth Street. I peered down the street. "Where's the stable?" All I could see were apartment buildings, a parking garage, and something that looked like a school. There was nothing on the block to suggest a stable.

Debbie sniffed the air and wrinkled her nose. "Make no mistake," she said, "it's around here somewhere."

We continued down the block.

"There it is!" Toni was bouncing up and down in excitement.

We stopped in front of an old building that looked more like a garage than a barn. But the sign above the door clearly said CLAREMONT RIDING ACADEMY.

Toni started to head up the dirt ramp that led off the sidewalk, but before she had even gone three steps, John grabbed the back of her shirt.

"Whoa there, Toni."

She reluctantly turned to face him.

"This is just a visit, a tour, so . . ." John started to say something else, but sneezed instead.

He reached into his pocket for a handkerchief, blew his nose, and continued. "This is just a tour, so . . ."

He sneezed again.

"Are you catching a cold, John?" Debbie asked.

"No," he said. He looked at Toni. "So I don't want you four to . . ."

He stopped, and sniffed. "I don't want you four to . . . ah-*choo!*"

"Are you sure you feel okay?" Debbie said.

"It might be allergies," John said. "Sometimes I— ah-*choo!*"

"That's terrible, John." Toni was all concern as she guided a sneezing John across the street and sat him down on a bench. I smiled, and watched as Debbie handed him a tissue from her purse.

"You stay right out here in the fresh air," Toni said as John wiped his watering eyes. "We'll just go in the office and ask some questions about the barn and be right out again. It is a historic building, after all."

I could see by the look on John's face that he was not convinced.

"Please, John, maybe they'll let us see the horses."

"I want to see where they live."

"I bet people come by to look all the time."

We all spoke at once, and as usual, when we joined forces, there was no way to resist.

"All right," John said, sniffling loudly. "I'll wait right here."

"I'll wait with you," Debbie said, sitting down next to him.

Letitia, meanwhile, hadn't said a word.

"C'mon, Letitia." I pulled her arm. "Maybe they have a horse like Grandpa's here. Remember, he was so big we both could ride him at the same time."

Letitia pulled her arm away.

"I'm not going in."

"C'mon, Allison." Toni, Susette, and Rosina had already crossed back over to the barn. "Let's go."

"Why not?" I argued. "You love horses as much as I do. Or at least, you did."

"Well, I don't anymore." Letitia's tone was final.

"Why *not?*" I wasn't ready to give up yet.

"Look, Allison," Letitia said, yanking her arm away. "There's no point in liking anything too much. You only end up disappointed." She turned and walked back toward Debbie and John.

I stood in the middle of the sidewalk and stared at her retreating back. What had she meant by *that?*

"Allison!" Toni was tapping her foot impatiently.

With one last look at my cousin, I crossed the street and joined my friends at the entrance to the barn.

Susette peered into the small dirt arena where seven or eight riders on horseback walked and trotted. There were four or five people standing in the middle of the arena, each yelling out instructions to a different rider.

I joined Susette next to the ring.

"Where do the horses live?" she whispered.

"Step back, girls. Can't you see there are lessons in progress?" A short woman with long curly hair motioned us back from the edge of the arena.

"Where can we find out about riding?" Toni called to the woman as she walked back toward the center of the ring.

"Right behind you, in the office." The woman turned her attention to the small girl on a big fat horse. "Okay, Megan, tell him to trot now."

We followed Toni into the office. It looked a little run-down, but had a really comfortable feel to it, like it had been around for a long time. Photographs of horses hung on the walls, and two huge cats, one gray and one orange, were sacked out in patches of sunshine near the windowsill.

A woman with long brown hair and glasses, who reminded me a little of Mrs. Freundlich, my fifth-grade English teacher, looked up as we stood by the counter.

"May I help you?"

"Yes, we'd like to rent some horses." Toni was not going to waste any time pretending to be interested in a tour of the place. We had a mission.

"So, did you want to schedule lessons, or a hack?"

A hack? I glanced at Toni, who looked momentarily confused.

"A hack." Rosina spoke firmly and stepped up to the counter.

"That means a ride in the park," she muttered to Toni.

"Do you all have previous riding experience? Is there an adult with you who can sign the permission forms?"

"I've been taking lessons for about six years," Rosina continued confidently. "I've shown and can jump. I'm sure our chaperone can sign the release forms. Would that be okay?"

I gave Rosina an admiring look. She was always so poised with adults.

"Well . . ." The woman took off her glasses and looked us over carefully. "What about you three?" She included Toni, Susette, and me in her inquiring gaze.

"I've ridden before," I answered truthfully. "I'm pretty good."

"Only a few times," Susette spoke up. "And I'm a little nervous."

Toni drew herself up to her full height and peered over the top of the counter. "I'm an expert rider. I guess I could ride just about any horse."

We all smiled. Toni's tendency to exaggerate had become so common to us, we just assumed that *everyone* could tell when she was stretching the truth.

"Here are the release forms." The woman handed us four sheets of paper. "Fill out both sides and have an adult sign the back. Then we'll talk about what horse would be right for each of you."

I could hardly contain my excitement. I was going horseback riding! And in New York City, of all places. That is, if John would let us.

I don't think I've ever wanted so badly to do anything before, and maybe John could tell, because he barely put up a fight before agreeing to let us ride. Despite his allergies, he insisted on coming into the office to speak to the woman behind the desk. And somehow, in between sneezes, he managed to sign the permission forms.

"Now—ah-*choo!* Don't you four go and do anything . . . ah-*choo!* . . . reckless or anything."

It was kind of hard to take him seriously when he was sneezing after just about every word.

"I think you'd better go back outside and wait with Debbie and Letitia," Toni told him. "You're going to scare the horses. We'll be fine. Trust me."

I thought John might reconsider right then and there, but he started sneezing like crazy again and just headed outside, shaking his head and wiping at his nose.

We handed the forms over to the woman behind the desk, who studied them carefully. She looked us over one more time.

"Pick out a helmet from those shelves." She pointed across the room at little cubbyholes that held velvet-covered riding caps. "And then come back and see me about which horse you'll be riding."

We each grabbed a helmet, and Rosina showed us how you had to be careful that the helmet fit snugly.

"Why do we even *need* helmets?" Toni asked.

"That sidewalk out there is pretty hard," the woman responded. "And you've got to ride the horses through the streets on the way to the park. It would be foolish not to protect yourself in case of a fall."

"Well, it's not like that's going to happen," Toni said.

But I could see that she checked her helmet one more time.

We lined up in front of the desk again.

"When I've told you which horse you're riding, you'll go out into the ring. The horses come from upstairs and downstairs, and you'll wait by the ramp near where your horse lives. Lead your horse into the middle of the ring and make sure the saddle is secure." She smiled at us. "My name is Judith. If you need help, you can ask Jackie or Florence." She pointed at two women, one with long dark hair and one with short blond hair, who stood talking in the center of the arena.

Rosina got a horse called Hoedown; Susette had a big handsome buckskin named Drifter; Toni was riding a horse called Tuskers; and I had a little chestnut named Napa.

We mounted the horses and the staff helped us fix our stirrups to the right length. Susette looked a little nervous, but Jackie told her that Drifter was one of the nicest horses in the stable. "He'll take perfectly good care of you. Just enjoy your ride in the park."

Rosina was the first one ready. "Let's go, you guys."

"Yee-ha!" I said. I was so excited to be on a horse again—it felt so natural. I decided I would look into riding lessons when I got home.

Toni was the last one ready. Her horse kept moving around as she tried to adjust the stirrup length.

One of the instructors walked up to her. "You must

be a pretty good rider. Tuskers used to be a race horse. He can be a handful in the park."

Toni turned a little pale. I rode over next to her. "You going to be okay?"

Toni nodded. "Sure," she said. "This horse really seems to like me."

Rosina led the way out of the stable, and then suddenly, there we were. Riding horses, right out into the middle of New York City traffic!

Taxi cabs were whizzing by at about the level of my knee, but the horses ignored them. I guess they were pretty used to this. Staying single file, with Rosina first, Toni second, me third, and Susette bringing up the rear, we walked to the end of the block, turned right and then right again, heading in a straight line to the park. I kept turning around to make sure Susette was all right.

These horses sure knew what they were doing. Every time we got to a red light, they stopped and stood patiently. Once we got into the park, we pulled up alongside each other.

"This is the nicest horse." Rosina reached over and patted Hoedown's neck. She seemed more relaxed and happy than I'd ever seen her.

"Here's to the Adventurers," Toni said as we began walking along the bridle path.

"*Just* the Adventurers," Rosina said pointedly, looking at me.

As if I needed to be reminded that I had more fun when Letitia wasn't around!

"I've got to admit, I like it better when your gloomy cousin isn't around," Rosina added.

"I got your point the first time," I replied. "Gloomy or not, she *is* my cousin."

"Besides, we think we may know why she's in such a bad mood all the time," Toni put in.

We let the horses walk along quietly as Toni and I told the other two the little we knew about the mysterious Malcolm.

"She always seems to be holding something back," Susette said thoughtfully. "Maybe it's not that she's unfriendly, just defensive."

I thought about that for a moment, and nodded.

"It does seem like finding out about Malcolm is the key to finding out about Letitia," I said. "But I don't know how we can do that."

"Don't worry, Allison," Susette replied, smiling. "We'll help you get back the cousin you remember."

I had a really warm feeling as I smiled at my friends. We had started our trip barely knowing each other, and now we were becoming a lot like family.

We came around a corner just then and found ourselves looking at a long straight stretch of bridle path.

"That's enough about Letitia for now," I said.

"Yeah, cowboy," Toni said, looking back at me. "Let's ride!"

We kicked our horses into a trot, laughing and yelling.

"This is the best!" I heard Susette cry behind me. Her nervousness seemed to have disappeared completely.

We trotted for maybe a minute. Up ahead, I could see Toni was having a little bit of trouble keeping Tuskers from running ahead of Rosina's horse.

"Whoa!" I heard her shout several times.

Rosina pulled her horse back to a walk, and waited for the rest of us to catch up.

"Tuskers is fast," I said to Toni, coming up alongside them.

She nodded. "He's a race horse, he must like to be first."

We waited for Susette to catch up. She had a big smile on her face. "Jackie was right," she said. "I really feel like this horse is taking care of me."

"Good," Rosina said, easing her horse into a walk. We were on a pretty wide stretch of path now, wide enough so that we could walk four abreast.

"You ride well, Toni," Rosina said. *"Especially* for someone who's never taken any lessons."

I saw a gleam come into Toni's eye. She hated to be challenged.

"I'm a natural," she replied.

"Do you want to try cantering?" Rosina asked.

Toni nodded. "Sure."

"All right, then," Rosina said, leaning forward. "Let's go!"

She took off like a shot, and a split second later Toni and Tuskers followed.

"Yeah!" I yelled, as Napa followed them. It was the best feeling in the world, cantering along a wide sunny path, on a horse, in the middle of New York City!

Up ahead, Toni passed Rosina. I could see both of them leaning even farther forward, urging their horses on. Rosina passed Toni again. They were really going all out, I realized. When had they decided to turn this into a race?

And then suddenly I got a little nervous. The path began to get a little narrower, the trees a little thicker. I eased Napa back a bit.

"I think we ought to slow down, guys!" I yelled. But they were too far off to hear me.

I turned around and saw Susette straining to maintain control of her horse.

"Just relax," I yelled back to her. I turned forward again, and then—

Everything seemed to happen at once.

Up ahead, Rosina was a few lengths in front of Toni. I saw the path split in two. Rosina went one way, Toni the other, down a narrower more wooded trail. I could see what she planned to do, to go fast enough to be past Rosina when the paths joined up again—

And then suddenly, Tuskers reared up, and Toni tumbled to the ground.

"Toni!" I screamed. Tuskers's front hoof landed inches away from Toni's head. He looked like he was ready to rear up again.

"Roll out of the way, Toni!" I urged Napa forward,

down the wooded trail. I saw Rosina stop and look back. A look of horror crossed her face. Toni didn't move.

Before I could reach her, a boy I hadn't seen a moment ago raised his arm to grab Tuskers's reins. But he was too slow. By the time I reached the two of them, Tuskers was galloping down the wide path as if he was on the backstretch.

But I really didn't care. Rosina rode up and jumped off her horse. There were tears streaming down her face. "I killed her! It's all my fault. I shouldn't have made her race."

The boy crouched over Toni, staring from one of us to the other.

Susette joined us. "Is she all right?"

The boy felt Toni's neck. "She has a pulse, so she's alive." He spoke directly to Rosina, who stopped sobbing and tried to compose herself.

Suddenly Toni opened her eyes. "Of course I'm alive."

She tried to sit up, but moaned and fell backward. "What happened?"

"Stay still," I said, dismounting quickly and bending over Toni. She was moaning and holding her right shoulder. But she didn't look as pale anymore.

"This idiot jumped right out in front of us," she said. "He scared Tuskers to death—"

"I think she'll be all right."

"I don't know," I said. "Rosina, Susette, I think you'd better go back to the barn and get an ambulance. Do you think you can lead Napa back with you?"

"Where's Tuskers?" Susette asked.

"He's probably headed home," the boy said. "I've seen stuff like this happen to riders before."

"Oh, no!" I said, swinging around to see if anyone had Napa. "This is terrible!"

I had visions of the two horses disappearing entirely—and of our trip being canceled once John found out that Toni had been hurt racing in the park.

"We'll tell them everything is going to be okay," Rosina said, turning her horse around. She held her reins in one hand, and was going to lead Napa back with her.

"I'll go with you," Susette said. They both headed down the path at a steady trot, and then they were gone from sight, and the three of us—me, Toni, and the boy who'd spooked her horse—were left alone.

"I'm sorry," the boy said. "I'm so sorry. I was so absorbed in drawing, and your friend came roaring down the trail right at me, and—"

"It's not your fault," I said. "They were going too fast."

"We were *not* going too fast," Toni said. "You were hiding."

"You were going too fast," I repeated. I turned to the boy. "Really. It's not your fault." I smiled at him, and for the first time, I noticed his stained jeans and dirty T-shirt.

He lives here, I realized suddenly. He lives in the park.

I was looking at a real live homeless person.

"I'm Allison," I said, holding out a hand and, for the

first time, looking at him closely. He was a few years older than us, with short hair and a pretty cute smile. For a stranger, there was something awfully familiar about him.

"I'm Malcolm," he said, taking my hand and shaking it. "Pleased to meet you."

I nodded. "And I'm pleased to meet you—at last."

Eight

"At last?" Malcolm looked at me strangely. "What do you mean by that?"

I shook my head, unsure where to begin. How could I explain everything that had happened over the last few days?

"I think we have a mutual friend," I began. "You see, my cousin—"

"Allison! Are you all right?"

I looked up. Letitia was standing at the top of the little hill where the two branches of the path came together again.

"I saw Rosina and Susette come out of the park leading your horses!" She was running down the hill toward us, talking at the same time. "And I wondered if—"

She stopped suddenly, when she got about ten feet away.

"Malcolm," she said quietly.

He stared at her. "Hey, Tish."

"Did somebody say Malcolm?" Toni asked, trying to sit up.

"Take it easy," I said, putting a hand on her shoulder. She still looked a little woozy.

"You're still here," Letitia said. Her voice, her whole manner was different. Gentle, almost. If Malcolm wasn't her boyfriend, he was sure very important to her.

"It's not like I have anyplace else to go," he replied.

She shook her head. "You know that's not true. You can always come back to Restart."

He shook his head. "Not now I can't. You know that." He looked at me again. "You two know each other."

"This is my cousin from California," Letitia replied. "And her friend."

"You look kind of familiar to me," Malcolm said. "Have we met before?"

I shook my head.

Letitia took a step closer to him. "Malcolm, come back," she said, as if Toni and I weren't there. "I'm sure we can figure out a way to keep you at Restart."

He shook his head. "I'm through with all the moving around, Tish. This is where I live now." He sounded sad, but determined. "I don't want to talk about it anymore."

"Fine. We won't," Letitia said, and suddenly her manner changed. She was back to being the Letitia who couldn't find anything nice to say about anyone. "We won't talk about anything."

"Tish," he said. "Don't be like that—"

"Listen, Malcolm, if you want to ignore your friends, run away from your problems . . ." Her voice caught in her throat.

I thought my cousin might be about to cry.

Malcolm lowered his head, and put his hands in his pockets. "What else can I do?" he said softly. "I *can't* come back."

I wanted to ask a million questions. Why couldn't Malcolm go back to Restart? What was this about a lot of moving around? And was he really living in Central Park?

"Then go," Letitia said. She turned away from him, and looked at Toni. "What happened to her?"

"Her horse bucked," I said. "I don't think there's anything broken."

"Let me have a look," Letitia said, kneeling down next to her.

And totally ignoring Malcolm.

"You know where I am, Tish," he said. Then he turned to me and managed a half-smile. "I hope your friend's okay. It was nice meeting you."

"Wait!" I said. "Don't go!"

"Leave him alone!" Letitia said. "If he wants to turn his back on everyone, let him!"

"I'm going, Tish," Malcolm said to her. "But I'll be back. I know where to find you, too."

And before I could say another word, he turned and began walking up over the hill. I watched him disappear over the rise.

"What's going on, Letitia?" I asked, kneeling down next to my cousin, who had helped Toni up into a sitting position. "What happened to Malcolm? Why isn't he at Restart anymore?"

"I don't want to talk about it," she snarled, looking up at me. I was startled at the anger in her voice. "I do *not* want to talk about it, okay? He's a jerk!"

Then my cousin turned back to Toni, and held up two fingers. She waved them in front of Toni's face. "Look at me, Toni. Focus on my hand."

"What are you doing?" I asked.

Letitia looked up at me. "No concussion." She turned to Toni. "Where does it hurt?"

"Just my shoulder, really," Toni said. "Oh, no, I've got a bruise on my forehead, don't I? I'm going to look like somebody beat me up."

"Your hair will cover it," Letitia said. "Besides, it's not even a bruise, really. The ground around here is so soft, you won't even get any discoloration." She frowned. "I want to take a look at your shoulder."

She began lightly pressing on Toni's right shoulder with both hands.

"Hey—do you know what you're doing?" I asked.

"When you have to look after half a dozen small kids during the day, you'd better know something about first aid," Letitia said. She helped Toni into a sitting position. "Here. Let me have your right arm, now. Relax. Relax."

"So that's the famous Malcolm," Toni said, looking off at the wooded part of the park that Malcolm had disappeared into. "Talk about a small world."

Letitia ignored her. "Hold still," she said, putting one arm on Toni's right shoulder. With the other, she rotated her arm slowly back and forth.

"Maybe not so small," I said, looking down at my cousin. "That's why you didn't want to go riding, isn't it? You knew we might run into Malcolm."

Letitia ignored me. "Does that hurt?" she asked Toni.

"A little sore, but no big deal," Toni said.

Letitia nodded and got to her feet. "Just a bruise. It'll hurt for a week or so, but you'll be fine."

"What about Malcolm?" I pressed.

Letitia turned to me and glared. "What about him?"

I glared right back at her. "Don't play dumb. What's he doing in the park? Is he really living here? Why?"

"He's not living here," Letitia said.

"But then why did he say he was?" I asked. Something was fishy.

"Look, I don't want to talk about it, all right?" she said. Just then, John and Debbie and Susette and Rosina appeared, full of questions and concerns.

"I'm okay, really," Toni said. "You can ask Letitia. My shoulder's just a little sore."

"She won't need an ambulance, or anything." Letitia got to her feet. "She just has a bruise on her shoulder. It'll be sore for a while, but there's no damage."

"Yeah," Toni chimed in. She turned to Rosina. "I was winning, you know."

Rosina shook her head. "You were not."

Toni smiled sweetly. "I'm ready to try it again if you are."

"Oh, no you're not." John stepped forward and shook his head. "There'll be no more unsupervised activity in the future. I don't know what I was thinking, letting you go off by yourselves like that. From now on, Debbie or I will stay with you at all times when you're out in the City. Are we clear on that?"

He folded his arms across his chest, glaring at each of us in turn until we each nodded.

When we got back to the hotel, there was a message waiting for us from Sara, asking if we would mind Letitia's staying over another night. Nobody seemed too thrilled, but now that I'd actually met Malcolm, I was more anxious than ever to find out more about him. Maybe if I could get my cousin alone again . . .

And then I got an even better idea.

"We're leaving for dinner in fifty minutes," John said. He and Debbie were standing in the hall, just outside the door of our room. We were planning to try a French restaurant that night. He turned to Toni.

"You're sure you're all right? We don't have to go out if you're not feeling up to it. We could stay here and watch cable, maybe order a pizza. . . ."

Toni shook her head firmly. "I'm fine. It's just my—"

"You *are* looking a little pale," I interrupted.

Everybody turned and stared at me. Toni looked fine, of course.

"Maybe you should stay here," I continued. "Get some rest."

"Hmmm." Debbie stepped into the room and looked at her sister closely. "I don't know, Allison. She looks all right to me."

Toni stared up at me—and I raised an eyebrow.

Toni got the message immediately. She wasn't my closest friend for nothing.

"I *am* feeling a little tired, I guess. I *could* stay here— if I had some company," she said.

"I never did like French food," I announced. Actually, I'd never had it before, but there would be other chances, I was sure. Like when we went to Paris. "I'll stay with you, if you want."

"Sure," Toni said. "We can get pizza."

I smiled.

It wasn't hard to convince John. And less than an hour later, Toni and I were alone in our room.

"I thought they'd never leave," Toni said. She sat up in bed. "So what's up?"

"We are," I said, climbing off my bunk. "We're up and out of here."

"Huh?"

"Let's go to the park. To find Malcolm again."

"What are you talking about?" Toni finally turned away from the TV and looked directly at me. "This is New York City. There are, like, ten million people who live here. You think we can just go outside and find one of them in Central Park? You're crazy!" She shook her head. Then a little gleam came into her eye. "You just think he's cute."

I ignored her teasing. "He said he lives there, right? What harm could it do to go back to where we saw him."

Toni shook her head. "I don't know . . ."

"Come on," I said, popping off the bed. "Have you lost your sense of adventure, Adventurer?"

She looked down at me. "Not on your life," she said. "Let's go." And she hopped down off her own bed.

And immediately cried out in pain and grabbed her shoulder.

"I completely forgot," I said, clapping my hand to my mouth. "You just fell off a horse!"

"I'm fine," Toni said. "Besides . . ." She smiled. "I'm getting a little hungry. Maybe we can find another one of those hot-dog vendors."

I nodded. "You read my mind."

We left a note for everybody, saying that Toni was feeling so much better that we'd gone out for a walk, and that we'd be back by seven thirty. It was barely six now. I figured we had plenty of time.

We quickly found the bridle path, and the spot where Toni had fallen. But there was no sign of Malcolm.

"Malcolm!" I called. "Malcolm—where are you? It's Toni and Allison."

"Hello! Malcolm!" Toni chimed in. She turned to me. "He's not here."

"Who's not here?"

I looked up to see a policeman walking down the bridle path toward us.

"What's the matter, girls?" he said. "Lose something?"

"Uh, not exactly," I said. "We're looking for—our cat."

Toni's eyes went wide.

"Maybe I can help you," the policeman offered. "What kind of cat is he?"

"Uh . . ."

"Siamese," Toni said.

"Yeah, Siamese," I said.

"All right." The policeman nodded. "What color?"

"White," I said.

"Black," Toni answered simultaneously.

We looked at each other.

"Black and white," I said finally.

"A black and white Siamese," the policeman repeated. "I'll keep an eye out for him."

"Her," Toni said. "He's a she. I mean, she's a girl."

"Of course she is." The cop nodded. "But even if you don't find him—or her—don't stay out here too much longer," he warned us. "You don't want to be in the park after dark."

"Right," I said. "We know that."

He walked away, disappearing around a bend.

Toni folded her arms across her chest and frowned.

"A cat?" She shook her head. "What possessed you to say that?"

"I have no idea," I said, turning off the bridle path. "Come on—Malcolm went this way. Maybe we can find him."

"Or our cat," Toni said.

We walked on in silence for a few minutes, getting deeper into the park. The path we were on gradually curved back and forth, till I felt I might be losing my bearings. But the setting sun gave me a landmark to work off.

"This is almost like being in a real forest," Toni said as we crossed over a little footbridge into a wooded area. "But I don't know that we're getting any closer to finding Malcolm."

I nodded. She was probably right, but . . .

"Let's just look a few minutes longer," I said. "I hate to give up now."

I really wanted to find out what was going on—and I had the sneaking suspicion that getting Malcolm to talk about what had happened to him would be a lot easier than getting Letitia to lower her defenses and talk about it.

The trees around us were getting taller and taller. Tall enough that they blocked out the buildings surrounding us. Up ahead, I could hear the sound of rushing water. For a moment it was loud enough to drown out the sounds of the city around us.

Then the path curved abruptly, and we found ourselves looking down at a little stream about fifty feet below us. A waterfall opposite us fed into the stream, and there were steps carved into the rocks ahead of us, leading down to it.

"Check it out," I said. "A miniature Grand Canyon."

"Cool."

We followed the path down, at one point going right

past the waterfall. I would have tried to reach out and touch it, but the rock underneath my feet was pretty slippery.

"Careful here," I said, turning back to Toni. "It's kind of—"

My left foot slipped.

"Allison!" Toni cried out.

I grabbed onto the guardrail—and my right foot caught on the rock, folding up underneath me.

"Ow!" I yelled. Pain shot up my leg.

"Are you okay?" Toni said, coming to my side. I regained my balance, holding on to the guardrail with both hands.

"I don't know," I said. "I might have twisted my ankle. Let me try putting a little weight on it. . . ."

I took a step forward—and almost collapsed again, the pain was so intense. I reached out for the nearest support, which happened to be Toni's shoulder.

The shoulder she'd hurt riding.

"Ow!" she said. She twisted away, and slipped—

And we both fell on our butts onto the hard, wet rock.

I was too stunned to say anything for a moment. I sat there, the water soaking through the back of my pants, and tears came to my eyes.

"Ow," I said. "Ow, ow, ow."

"Double ow," Toni agreed, slowly getting to her feet. "My pants are soaked." She looked down at me, and held out her left hand. "Let's try that again."

I grabbed her hand, got to my feet, and took a hesitant

step forward. This time, I was prepared for the pain, and managed a couple of steps before stopping.

"It hurts!" I cried.

"Can you walk?"

"I can limp." I looked up at the way we'd come. I noticed that it was almost dark.

How had it gotten so late?

Suddenly the woods around us seemed a little scary.

"Let's get out of here," Toni whispered.

"You read my mind," I said. Now the sun had disappeared entirely, and my sense of direction was completely gone. As was my desire to find Malcolm. I was cold, wet, hurt, and wanted nothing more than to be back in our little hotel room, safe in my bed. Maybe Letitia would talk to me tomorrow.

On the path up ahead, Toni turned around and frowned at me. "Come on!" she urged.

"I can only go so fast," I said. "I think my ankle—"

Up ahead, I heard something snap. Like a twig underneath somebody's foot.

"What was that?" Toni asked.

"I don't know," I said honestly. "It sounded like—"

The crackling sound came again, louder this time.

"Somebody's coming," Toni said.

I nodded, visions of running into some crazy New York person dancing through my head.

What a *stupid* idea this was, to go walking through Central Park at night.

"Can't you go any faster?" Toni asked.

"Sorry, sorry," I said. "I can't walk and you can't help me." I sniffed once. I told myself I was *not* going to cry.

We were back to the edge of the woods. But—

"Where's the path?" I wondered out loud. It was pitch-black, and I was having a hard time seeing.

"This way," Toni said, heading off in one direction.

"No." I shook my head. "I think we came from the other direction."

"No," Toni said firmly. "I'm positive this is the right way—"

"Oh, terrific," I said. My ankle was killing me, and now I couldn't hold back the tears. "We're lost."

"We're not lost," Toni insisted. "We—"

The cracking sound came again—and now with it, I heard footsteps.

"It's definitely a person," I said. "It could be that policeman."

Toni shook her head. "Why would he be sneaking around like that? Here, quick!"

She grabbed my hand and half-dragged me off the path behind some trees. We sat down on the ground, both breathing heavily.

"Take this," Toni whispered.

She handed me a rock.

"What?" I said. "Are you crazy?"

"Me, crazy?" Toni said. "Whose idea was it to come here, anyway?"

I had no answer for that. So I held the rock tightly

in my hand, hoping whoever was out there would just go away.

But the footsteps kept getting louder. And closer.

"He can't know where we are," Toni said.

I nodded. Of course he couldn't. Soon he'd go past us, and—

The underbrush parted. Somebody was standing right above us, looking down.

I couldn't help it. I screamed.

Nine

"Stay back!" Toni yelled. "I'll hit you with this rock."

"Easy, easy," the stranger said, taking a step backward. I looked up—

"Hey," I said. "It's Malcolm!"

"It's Malcolm?" Toni said, lowering her hand.

"It's Malcolm," he agreed. "Allison, right?"

"Right," I said. "And you remember Toni."

He waved. "Hi, Toni."

"Hi, Malcolm."

He folded his arms across his chest. "Can I ask you guys a question? What are you doing here?"

"Oh, that," I said, climbing to my feet. "Ow. Well, actually, we were looking for you."

"Really?"

"Really." I sighed. "It's a very long story."

Before I could tell it, Malcolm led us out of the park. Maybe ten minutes later, we were sitting on a bench all the way over on Fifth Avenue, right near the Metropolitan Museum, eating hot dogs and drinking soda.

"This is great, guys," Malcolm said, biting into his second hot dog. "Thanks so much."

"Any friend of Letitia's is a friend of mine," I said. "You are a friend of Letitia's, aren't you?"

"Her boyfriend?" Toni pressed.

Malcolm laughed and shook his head. "No, I'm not her boyfriend. She's kind of like my kid sister more than anything else." He looked at me funny for a second, then snapped his fingers. "Allison! I know where I've seen you before."

"Huh?" I said.

"You're in that goofy-looking picture Letitia keeps in her album. You're the cousin who spent the summer in Mississippi with her, right?"

I smiled. "Guilty."

Malcolm nodded. "Right, I knew I recognized you. But you sure have changed. You're nowhere *near* as geeky-looking as you were then."

I felt myself beginning to blush.

"So where do you fit in Letitia's life?" Toni pressed.

"That's a long story," Malcolm said.

"It's what we want to hear," I said.

"Why?"

I turned to face him directly. "Because I think it has something to do with why Letitia seems so upset all the time."

Malcolm looked surprised. "Letitia?" He shook his head. "I know my leaving upset her, but still . . . She's one of the most level-headed, positive people I've ever met."

"What?" Toni and I blurted out simultaneously. Now it was my—no, our—turn to be surprised. "Are we talking about the same Letitia?" Toni asked.

"Wait, wait," I said, holding up a hand. "Start at the beginning."

Malcolm was suddenly quiet. "All right," he said finally, "but whatever I tell you stays between us, right?"

"Right," Toni and I promised.

"Okay," Malcolm said. He took a deep breath. "I think maybe Letitia's upset because I'm living here in the park."

"We got that," I said. "But *why* are you here?"

He looked away. "I guess the main reason is because I'm an orphan."

"Oh," Toni said, and I could hear in her voice the knowledge of what it felt like to grow up with only one parent. How much harder would it be to grow up with none?

"I heard you were at Restart, though," I said.

"Six years." Malcolm nodded. "My mom and I were there almost from the beginning. Then last year, when she left—"

"Your mom just *left* you?" Toni interrupted.

"That's right," Malcolm said, his voice flat. "For a year, I got to stay there with Letitia and Sara. Then the state decided I'd be better off with some foster parents." He leaned back against the bench, and shook his head. "So they sent me to this couple, the Mastersons, out in Queens. They lived in this big apartment project that was like . . ." He seemed at a loss for words. "Like your worst nightmare," he said finally.

"And?" I prompted.

"And after about a week with them, I ran away."

"Why?" Toni asked. "What—"

"I don't want to talk about that," he said. "Let's just say that I'm not going back there. Ever. And I can't go back with Aunt Sara and Letitia, because if the DSS finds me there, they'll get in trouble. Restart will get in trouble."

We all sat quietly for a moment, thinking. I was beginning to see the problem. "So what are you going to do? Live in the park forever?"

"No," he said. "Just until September first. Then I turn eighteen. Then I can do whatever I want."

"And what do you want?" I asked.

"Well . . ." Malcolm smiled. "I want to go to art school."

I remembered the painting I'd seen in the hallway at Restart.

"I got a scholarship to the summer seminars at Art-Space, but because I'm not eighteen and I don't have a legal guardian, I had to give it up," Malcolm said.

"But how can you live in the park?" Toni asked.

"It's not so bad, really," he replied. "Usually I sleep during the day, because it is pretty safe then. I can lie out in one of the fields and catch a few good hours." He looked up at Toni. "Unless somebody almost runs me over with a horse."

"Sorry," Toni said. We giggled.

"It's all right," he said. "Then, when it gets to be dark, I either ride the subways, or if I've managed to get together some money, I'll go to a coffee shop and get something to eat. There's one over on Third Avenue that lets me stay from midnight right through the morning rush. I can do some sketching there."

"Cool," Toni said. I had to admit, Malcolm made it all sound kind of romantic.

"The *real* problem is clothes," he said. "And staying clean."

"How do you do that?" I asked.

"Well, a friend of mine got me a membership to a city pool. So I can go there every day and swim and take a shower." He smiled. "Maybe the DSS will let me live *there.*"

"The DSS? You said those initials before—what do they stand for?"

"Department of Social Services," Malcolm replied. "It's a state agency."

I frowned. DSS? It sounded awfully familiar to me.

"Got it," I said, snapping my fingers. The computer that I'd logged onto at Restart.

The computer that contained all the information about Malcolm.

I felt goosebumps run up and down my spine.

"Ally-Cat?" Toni asked. "Are you all right? Is it your ankle?"

"I'm fine," I said, smiling. "I think I have an idea."

I turned to Malcolm. "An idea that will make it so you can attend ArtSpace this summer, at least for the second half."

"Not that I doubt you—but *how* are you going to manage that?"

I shook my head. "I don't want to tell you—just yet. But it's in the bag. I promise."

Malcolm looked at Toni. "Is she serious?"

"I've seen this expression on her face before," Toni said staring at me. "She'll do what she's promised."

Malcolm shook his head from side to side. "Why would you go out of your way to help me?"

"I'm not doing it just for you," I replied. "I'm doing it for Letitia, too. Because seeing you safe—seeing you back home—is very important to her."

"You guys must be pretty close," Malcolm said.

"Actually, we're not," I replied. "But we're family." I got to my feet—slowly. "Come on, Toni. We've got a lot to do."

We arranged for Malcolm to meet us in front of our hotel at eight fifteen the next morning, and then set off at as fast a jog as I could manage on my injured ankle. My plan wouldn't work unless we got back before the others.

"Have a good dinner, girls?" the man at the front desk called to us as we came in.

"Fine thanks," I said, trying to catch my breath. "Are the others back?"

"Nope," he said, shaking his head.

"They will be soon. It's already eight o'clock," Toni said. "That's pretty late to still be at dinner."

"Late nothing," the man replied. "On *this* late shift, I don't get my dinner break until 11:00."

"Um, you must get really hungry," I babbled, heading for the elevator. Why did Toni have to start a conversation? We had to get back to the room and pretend we'd been there all the time.

We had just changed into our sweats and clicked on the TV when Letitia, Susette, and Rosina came bursting into the room, talking a mile a minute about dinner.

"John ate snails." Susette shuddered.

"Escargots," he corrected as he appeared in the doorway. "How are you feeling, Toni?"

"Better, thanks," Toni replied, trying to sound weak.

"You look flushed." Debbie came over and put a hand on her sister's forehead. "Are you sure you're fine?"

"Yes," Toni insisted, a note of irritation creeping into her voice.

"That sounds like the old Toni," Letitia said from behind Debbie and John's backs.

John grinned. "I'll be downstairs in the lounge, reading. Don't forget that we have an early day tomorrow morning. And Sara's coming at eight to meet Letitia."

He closed the door behind him.

"Seriously, Toni." Letitia flopped down on the love seat and clicked the TV from VH-1 to MTV. "Are you feeling okay?"

"Better than okay." Toni was suddenly animated. "We know all about Malcolm."

Letitia froze.

"And we can help him," I said before Letitia could reply. I filled everyone in on what we'd been doing while they were out to dinner.

And then I explained my plan.

"Are you crazy?" Letitia asked when I stopped for breath. "Number one, it's illegal. Number two, you can't just walk into a computer store and use their computers."

"I wasn't thinking of a computer store," I said.

"There are computers at Restart," Susette said slowly.

"Hold on a second," Rosina said. "Now what you're talking about is *doubly* illegal—breaking and entering *and* changing records."

"It's not breaking and entering if someone has keys," Toni said, looking right at Letitia.

"It's still breaking the law," Rosina snapped.

"Well, the law's not doing Malcolm a whole lot of good right now," Letitia said. She looked carefully at me. "Are you sure you can do this?"

"I can try," I said. "Whether or not it works . . ."

"I *know* you can do it, Ally-Cat," Toni said. "Come on, Letitia, let's give it a shot."

"I don't know," she said, shaking her head slowly. "Why do you want to help me? Why do you guys want to help Malcolm?"

"Because," I said, "it seems like he's had a lot of bad breaks. It's about time he got a good one."

"Yeah," Toni chimed in. "And we're just the Adventurers to give it to him!"

Letitia looked up at me, and I could have sworn she was smiling a little.

"All right," she said. "Let's give it a shot."

We were all sitting on our beds in the dark. We had agreed that we would leave the hotel around 11:00 P.M., sneak out to Brooklyn, change Malcolm's age in the files, and be back at the hotel in a couple of hours. The only thing we couldn't figure out was how to get out to Restart.

"It's getting awfully late to take a subway," Letitia said, glancing at the digital clock on the bureau.

"We can't leave any earlier," Toni whispered. "The guy at the front desk said he didn't get dinner break until eleven."

"That's the only time we can get out of here," I agreed.

"Why don't we just take a cab?" Rosina asked.

"A cab would cost about twenty dollars," Letitia said. "And with five of us going, we'd have to take two cabs. That's forty dollars."

"And back again, don't forget," I reminded her. *"Eighty* dollars."

"I have it," Rosina said.

"You have eighty dollars to spare?" Letitia shook her head. "Why not spend it on shopping or something?"

"This is what I want to spend it on," Rosina declared. "I'm not a computer expert like Allison, but I want to help Malcolm, too."

C'mon, Letitia, I thought silently. This is not time to be proud.

"Thank you, Rosina." Letitia's voice was full of emotion. "I can't thank you guys enough. You don't even really know Malcolm—or me—but you're willing to help us so much. I don't understand it."

"You're Allison's family," Susette said simply.

In the dark, I felt Letitia grab my hand and squeeze gently.

"Time to go," Toni said suddenly, breaking the weepy moment. She grabbed her Giants baseball cap and pulled her hair into a ponytail. "Let's get Malcolm into school!"

We stuffed our pillows and clothes under the covers on our beds; if John or Debbie peeked in before we returned, hopefully they'd think the lumps were us. Then we crept out into the hallway, closing the door gently behind us.

The hotel was totally silent. We headed for the elevator, but as Toni reached out to push the button, Rosina touched her arm.

"We better take the stairs," she whispered. "That old elevator starts up pretty noisily."

Letitia nodded and headed for the fire stairs at the end of the hall. We silently filed down the stairs and to the door leading out into the lobby. Susette cracked the door and peered out toward the desk.

"I'll go first and see if anyone notices me," she said. "If I can make it to the door, I'll give the all-clear sign and the rest of you can follow."

She eased her way out the door and began moving silently across the lobby. As she passed the front desk, she peered into the office in the back, then suddenly crouched down.

She motioned to us to follow, but signaled us to stay low, too.

Staying crouched down, we scuttled across the lobby and met up with her outside.

"Great work, Susette," Letitia said admiringly. "You've got a lot of nerve."

Hailing a cab was easy. Rosina got two to pull over right away and the next thing we knew we were on our way to Brooklyn.

I was in a cab with Toni and Rosina. You'd have thought we'd have plenty to talk about, considering what we were about to do. But except for a few comments about the traffic, we were all pretty silent. They were probably realizing what a stupid, dangerous plan I'd come up with, I decided. Me—stable old Allison—leading us into our shadiest adventure yet. What was I trying to prove?

I wanted to help Malcolm—and, by extension, Letitia. That much was true. But there was also part of me that wanted to show everybody—especially Letitia—

that I wasn't just some airhead rich girl from California, that I could pull my own weight anywhere, anytime.

Well, here's your big chance, Ally, I told myself. Just be sure you don't blow it.

Letitia had the cabs drop us off about a block away from Restart.

"We can sneak up better this way," she explained. "There's usually a night watchman on duty, but by now he should be asleep. He'll never hear us if we're quiet."

We tiptoed up the front path and around the back of the house. Letitia let us in with her key.

"Now be quiet," she said, putting a finger to her lips as she opened the door. "Even though most of the residents sleep on the third floor, sound carries in this house."

I nodded. "Lead on."

She flipped on the light switch and led me back to the computer.

"All yours," she said.

I flipped on the computer and waited for it to boot up. Then I ran the communications program and dialed up the same number I had dialed the day before. The same menu appeared again:

USER: RESTART
WELCOME TO
DSS
Please make your selection from the following menu:
A) Services Directory

B) Procedures & Guidelines
C) News
D) On-line Assistance

I hit the *D* key, and the menu changed.

I had figured On-line Assistance as the best place to start looking for ways into the DSS's own records. What I hadn't counted on was their computer being *so* ready to assist.

"This is too good to be true," I said, pointing at the menu. "Look."

This is what the screen displayed:

l) Edit Existing Client Information
2) Add new Client Information

"Wow," Toni said. "So all you have to do is call up Malcolm's record and edit it, right?"

"Wrong," I said. "I'll bet you money that you can't change a record that easily. But if we enter a new one . . ." I typed in *2,* and a blank information form came up on screen, with spaces for name, address, and a whole lot of other information—including birthdate.

Letitia frowned. "They're not just going to take your word for it about Malcolm, are they?"

"Probably not," I agreed. "They'll have to ask for a reference."

There was a blank for that, too. I filled in Letitia's name.

"Oh, you're devious," Letitia said, a light going on in her eyes.

"Thank you," I said. "Be expecting a call tomorrow."

"I'll be waiting by the phone all day," my cousin replied. "Oh, Allison, I don't know how to thank you—"

"Somebody's coming!" Susette hissed.

My heartbeat tripled. "What?" I looked at Letitia. "What do we do?"

"It must be the security guard!" she said, her eyes widening. "Hide!"

I looked around the office. The entire room was filled with desks, chairs, and filing cabinets. There wasn't a single closet to hide in or a couch to duck behind. "Where do you suggest?"

"Under the desk," Letitia said, grabbing me out of the chair and pushing me to the floor. "Hurry!"

A light came on in the hall.

"Anybody here?" I caught a glimpse of a short, skinny man in a uniform before I managed to squeeze myself under the desk—right next to Toni.

"Ow," she said. "Hey, find your own hiding spot. I was here first."

She looked ridiculous—her Giants hat was squishing her hair down so that it practically covered her face.

"It's the security guard," Letitia hissed. "Stay quiet."

I heard the sound of the door opening.

"Eddie," Letitia said, doing her best to sound surprised. I had to say, it was a good thing she wasn't hoping to be an actress. "What are *you* doing here?"

"I could ask you the same question, Letitia. This office is closed up."

I bent lower, trying to get a glimpse of the guard under the desk—and slammed my head into Toni's knee.

She stifled a giggle, and I glared at her.

"Well, to tell you the truth," Letitia said, "I left the keys to my house here."

Not a bad excuse on short notice. We'd make an Adventurer out of my cousin yet.

"Why couldn't you come get 'em tomorrow?" the watchman asked. He was coming closer, I realized. I elbowed Letitia in the knee. Get up, I thought furiously. If he comes around the desk, he'll see us and we're finished.

Letitia stood, and walked quickly toward him.

"My mom would kill me if she knew I wasn't taking care of my stuff. You can't tell her you found me here, Eddie," Letitia continued. "She'll never let me have any responsibility again."

"All right, Letitia," the man said. "I won't tell. But listen, you got to get out of here now. Get on back home."

"I will, in just a minute," Letitia said. "I just—"

"No justs, Miss," Eddie said. "You got to get on back home. It's too late for a young girl like you to be out." He paused a moment. "I know what I'm going to do. I'm going to get my daughter Sharon to come give you a ride. She lives just around the corner."

"No, Eddie, I'll be all right," Letitia said. "I can walk."

"Too late to walk," Eddie insisted. "Now come on."

"Hold on," she said. "I need my bag."

I heard her walking back toward us, and then suddenly she was bending down, less than two inches away from me.

"I think it's down here," she called back to Eddie. She made one of those "what can I do now?" faces at me.

I made one right back at her.

She frowned. "No, I guess not," she said, standing. "Oh. There it is. On that other desk."

"No wonder you always losing things," Eddie said. "You forget where you had 'em."

"I guess you're right, Eddie," Letitia replied, laughing. It sounded really forced. But Eddie laughed right back.

"I guess I'm right," he said. "Heh. Now let's go."

I heard them walking towards the door. Then the lights went out, the door shut, and their footsteps disappeared down the hall.

I waited another half-minute before getting out from under the desk. Toni unbent herself and squeezed out from behind me. Rosina and Susette emerged from underneath another desk, looking as rumpled as we probably did.

"That was close," Rosina said. She was smiling. "This is kind of exciting, isn't it?"

"*Kind* of," Susette said.

"It's a good thing we don't need your cousin anymore, right, Ally?" Toni asked. "I mean, we can just let ourselves out when you finish."

"You bet," I said, bending back to the computer. I

Suddenly Rosina snapped to attention.

"What's that noise?"

Susette dropped the book she was reading.

"It's coming from outside the window!"

"What if it's someone coming to steal the computer equipment?" Rosina picked up a baseball bat that one of the kids had left lying on the ground.

"It's coming from that window over there," Susette said, pointing.

We all stared, frozen, as a shadowy figure loomed up outside the window. The window began to slide open.

"Oh my God," Rosina said. "It's a burglar."

"And we're trapped!" Toni grabbed a paperweight off the desk. "I won't go down without a fight!"

My heart was racing. It was all my stupid fault. If I hadn't led us here . . . I took an involuntary step back as the stranger came into focus.

And then I smiled.

"Hey, Cousin," Letitia said, leaning through the open window. I grabbed her outstretched hand and helped her climb in. "Long time no see."

"Wait a minute," Rosina said, frowning. "You guys have a security guard—and you leave the window open."

"It's a habit," Letitia said. "One I started a long time ago."

Rosina looked at her strangely. I just smiled. Then Letitia explained, about the window, and about what had happened to her. She'd gone outside with the security guard and convinced him to let her take a cab home. Once she'd hailed one, of course, she'd simply had the driver take her around the block a couple of times and drop her off again.

"So how's it going?" Letitia asked.

"Pretty good," I said. "I'm just about done here."

"Good, because it's two thirty in the morning."

My eyes went wide. "Two thirty? Holy smokes!"

I made one final pass through the records, putting everything in the best possible order I could. I'd changed Malcolm's birthday, making him eighteen as of this very evening—which meant that he could move in with Sara and Letitia anytime he wanted, and go to art school if that's what he desired.

All he had to do was notify the DSS that he was exercising that right.

"I can't thank you enough," Letitia said. "If this works . . ."

"It's going to work," I said, shutting down the computer. "Now let's get out of here."

This time there was no argument about the transportation home. Letitia made a phone call to a neighborhood car service and we were back at the hotel at three fifteen. Which gave us about four hours of sleep before we had to meet Malcolm in the park.

"Just drop me on the floor," Toni groaned as we walked into the hotel. This time we didn't even bother sneaking past the man at the front desk. Not that we had to—he was fast asleep, slumped over the counter.

"Maybe we should just stay up," Rosina said.

"Not me." Susette shook her head. "I'm going to get my three hours."

"I'm with you," I said as we filed on the elevator and went up to our room.

"I think we pulled it off," I said as we all climbed into bed.

"We just have to find Malcolm now," Letitia said. "And tell him what the deal is."

I nodded. "That's right," I said. "Tell him what the deal is. . . ."

I heard my voice trailing off. There was something else I wanted to say. . . .

But the next thing I knew, it was morning. The sun was shining through our window, and everyone else was already up. Clothes and suitcases were scattered all over the room, and Toni sounded hysterical.

"It's not anywhere," she said. "Someone stole it."

"Who would want your hat?" Rosina said. "It's only a stupid baseball cap."

Toni planted her hands on her hips and turned to Rosina. "For your information, it is *not* stupid, and it is not *just* a baseball cap. It is—"

"Hey," I said, clearing my throat. "What's up?"

"Toni lost her hat," Rosina said.

"I didn't lose it, it was stolen," Toni corrected.

I frowned. "When did you last have it?"

"Sometime yesterday—I can't remember exactly when," she said. "I put it on to go riding, then—"

"You had it last night at Restart," I said suddenly. I remembered our squeezing under the desk . . .

"I had it at Restart," Toni said. "And then . . ." Her voice trailed off, and a panicked look crossed her face.

"Oh, no!" she exclaimed. "When I fell asleep on the floor—my hat must have fallen off!"

"You left it at Restart?" Rosina's eyes grew wide.

"You're kidding," Letitia said. "I don't believe it."

Toni moaned again. "If anybody finds it . . ."

"Don't worry," Susette said, trying to be helpful. "Maybe you actually left it in the cab."

"Or maybe it's just around here somewhere, and we can't find it in all this mess," I said.

"No," Toni said. "It's gone. I know it."

There was a knock on the door.

"Come in," Susette called.

The knob turned, and John stepped into the room.

"Let's move it, girls." He glanced around at our luggage. Then he shrugged and saw me still lying on my bunk. "Allison, come on. Get out of bed! Your aunt is already downstairs waiting for Letitia."

"All right," I said, hopping down. "I'll be just a second."

But fifteen minutes later we still weren't downstairs. So what if we were running a little late? The sun was shining outside, we had a full day of sightseeing ahead of us, and best of all, we were filled with the knowledge of the good deed we'd done last night.

All in all, it looked like things were A-okay this morning among the Adventurers.

And then, suddenly, they weren't.

The door swung open, and my aunt Sara walked in. "Girls. Can I talk to you all for a minute?"

"Sure," I said, trying to sound innocent though a boulder-sized knot had suddenly appeared in my stomach. "Come on in."

"I stopped by Restart this morning. And look what I found in the office," she said, holding out Toni's Giants cap.

Rosina was standing right behind me. I heard her draw in a breath, and a second later, whisper, "Oh my God, we're going to jail."

I turned and gave her a dirty look.

"That's your going-away present, Letitia!" Toni blurted.

"Uh, thanks," Letitia said.

"It's a nice sentiment," Aunt Sara said calmly. "But neither of you have been to Restart since two nights ago. And you were wearing the hat at my house later that evening, Toni, at dinner."

I looked over at my best friend, expecting to see her getting ready to reply with a smart remark.

Only she wasn't. She was just standing there, frozen.

"Toni?" Aunt Sara prompted. "I'm waiting."

"Umm . . ." Toni looked nervously over at me. "Uhh—"

My aunt followed Toni's gaze. "Allison? Can you tell me why Toni's hat was at Restart?"

My mind raced. What did my aunt know? What *could* she know? She couldn't know about what we'd done to help Malcolm. All she had was Toni's hat. All I had to do was explain *that*.

There was really no need to panic.

"And while you're thinking about how to answer *that*," Aunt Sara continued, "you should know that the hat wasn't the only thing waiting for me at the office this morning." She folded her arms across her chest. "There was an interesting phone call for you, Letitia. From the Department of Social Services."

Letitia and I exchanged a nervous glance.

"A message about Malcolm Cole. Wanting you to call them back and confirm his records—specifically his date of birth. Because he's going to ArtSpace this summer."

"He's going to ArtSpace?" Letitia repeated mechanically.

"Yes. If he can prove he's eighteen," Aunt Sara said.

"But he's only seventeen," Letitia said in the same wooden tone of voice.

"That's right," Sara replied. "But somehow, the DSS has it in their heads that he's already of age."

"Really?" My voice cracked.

My aunt nodded. "Really. It's even in their records." She stared right at me till I felt my knees begin to shake. "Now what do you suppose gave them that idea?"

I bowed my head, and swallowed hard. "Uhh . . ."

"Letitia? Susette? Any of you girls have anything to say?"

Next to me, Toni shuffled her feet nervously.

Aunt Sara began tapping her right foot on the floor quietly.

"I want answers, girls. And I'm going to get them—or none of you is going anywhere."

"I'm supposed to be at work, Mom," Letitia protested.

"John and Debbie will be here any second," I added. "Then we'll have to go sightseeing."

Aunt Sara shook her head. "Am I not making myself clear? You, Letitia, are one step away from being grounded for the entire summer. And the rest of you are one step away from having the remainder of your trip canceled!"

"But you can't do that!" Rosina exclaimed.

Aunt Sara raised a finger and shook it at her. "Don't you think that for a second, young lady."

I'd never seen my aunt so mad. And I couldn't remember ever being so nervous.

There was only one way out of this. The truth.

I took a deep breath, and stepped forward. "It's my fault, Aunt Sara. I did it. I changed the computer files so that Malcolm was on record as being older than he really is."

My aunt's mouth dropped open. "You—"

"No, no, it was me, Mom, I made her do it," Letitia cried.

I shook my head. "No, it was—"

There was a knock on the door.

"It's Debbie," Toni said. "I'm sure—"

The door swung open, and a bellboy walked in. One step behind him was Malcolm.

"Hail, hail, the gang's all here," Toni said quietly.

I checked my watch. Eight fifteen.

I had completely forgotten Malcolm was meeting us here.

"I hope I'm not disturbing you ladies," the bellboy said. "I caught this guy hanging around out front, and I thought he was going to cause trouble. But he said he knew one of you—"

"It's all right," Aunt Sara said. "He's with us."

The bellboy nodded and walked out, shutting the door behind him.

"Aunt Sara," Malcolm said, looking around the room. "Letitia. What are you all doing here?"

"I could ask the same thing of you," Sara replied.

"She told me to come here," Malcolm said, pointing at me. He frowned. "Say, you haven't done anything to—"

"All right," Sara said, raising her hands. "Allison, I want to hear the whole story now. From the beginning."

I sighed. My brainstorm for getting Malcolm into ArtSpace had turned out to be a *really stupid* brainstorm. Not only had I failed to accomplish my goal, but I had gotten my cousin in so much trouble that she'd probably never talk to me again. And I'd probably gotten the rest of our summer vacation canceled. Once John and Debbie found out what we'd done . . .

I took a deep breath, and told Aunt Sara the whole story.

When I finished, my aunt stared at me a moment. Then she spoke.

"You'll call the DSS and tell them what you did," she said.

"Right away," I said, feeling miserable.

She turned to Letitia. "You'll tell Eddie you lied to him."

My cousin nodded, and lowered her head.

Finally, Aunt Sara turned to Malcolm.

"And you'll move in with Letitia and me, and start attending ArtSpace right away."

Malcolm's eyes went wide. "What?"

I wasn't sure I'd heard right either.

"You heard me," Sara replied. "I want you to move in with us."

Malcolm shook his head. "I can't do that. I can't take charity anymore. I told you that before."

"You'd *rather* live in the park?" Rosina asked.

"That's right," Malcolm replied. "I'm tired of people feeling responsible for me. I don't want to be a burden on anyone—ever again."

"You see, Mom," Letitia said, her voice tight with emotion. "He won't let people do anything for him."

"I understand what you're feeling, Malcolm," Aunt Sara replied. "But you should realize that you won't be a burden to me—or to Letitia."

"Everybody always says that!" There was anger in Malcolm's voice—the first such emotion I'd heard. "My mom said that."

"Well, I'm not your mom," Aunt Sara replied quietly.

"But I'd like you to think of us, Letitia and me, as family."

Malcolm was silent for a moment as he digested Sara's words.

"I don't know," he said finally. "I just don't like the idea of taking charity."

"Oh, it won't be charity, Malcolm," Sara replied, putting her hands on her hips. "You'll be earning your keep for the summer. For one, I need someone to paint the entire office, inside and out."

Malcolm smiled. "Sounds like a busy couple of months."

"Months?" Sara shook her head. "I'm just talking about your first *week.*"

"So? What do you say?" Letitia asked, her voice almost shy.

Malcolm's smile widened. "I guess I say—yes."

"Yes!" Letitia whispered.

"Maybe we can help you with some of that work," Rosina said. "After all, I don't think we're going to be doing much of anything else this summer, once John and Debbie find out what we did last night."

"Why, are you going to tell them?" Aunt Sara asked. She was smiling.

"You're not going to tell John—or Debbie?" Toni asked in disbelief.

"No—I'm not," Aunt Sara replied.

"But why?" I blurted.

"Because you're family, honey," she said. "And we have got to stick together, no matter what."

I felt tears come to my eyes. "Oh, Aunt Sara." She opened her arms, and I ran into them. Just the way I'd begun the visit to New York.

Only this time, I looked past her to see Letitia—my cousin.

She was crying, too.

I broke free of Sara's embrace and hugged Letitia.

"That goes for all the rest of you, too," Sara said. "I consider you all part of my family, now. That means you have to write to me when you leave here."

"We will," I heard Susette say.

"Well, *this* looks like an emotional scene." I looked up to see John and Debbie standing in the doorway, staring at all of us. "I hope we're not interrupting."

"Not at all," Aunt Sara said. "Just having a little reunion here." She introduced Malcolm.

"Well," John said. "Sounds like cause for a celebration."

"Sylvia's makes a great brunch," Letitia put in. "The French toast is incredible."

John smiled. "That sounds right up my alley." Then he frowned. "I wonder if they have a table big enough for all of us."

"They will," Aunt Sara replied. "It's a family-style restaurant."

"Perfect," I said, looking around the room at everyone. "Because what we have here is a family."

Dear Mom,
    Well . . . a relatively uneventful time in New York

City, at least compared to the Grand Canyon, or Maine. I do have stories to tell, of course, but they're the kind I can save for when I get home.

I guess the most important thing about this trip is a lesson I feel I learned. And that is: No matter how many miles separate you, no matter how long between visits you go, family is the one thing in this life that you can count on.

I can think of you, and Dad, and the boys, and know that there's somebody out there that will be there for me, no matter what. And now, I guess I feel that way about Letitia and Sara, too. (And also about Toni, and Rosina, and Susette!)

And oh yeah—tell Robby thanks for teaching me so much about computers. He can count on my next letter being for him.

Miss you—

Love,
Allison

Hello!

Do it! You have to go to New York and ride in Central Park. It's so amazing!

I learned to horseback ride at Claremont Stables when I moved to New York to go to Columbia University at eighteen. Within a couple of years I was teaching there, and I swear, my happiest times have been spent in that barn or in Central Park.

I've also taught riding in England. Riding anywhere is a blast (plus it's really good exercise for the legs and tush). I think that's one of my favorite things about riding—you can do it anywhere in the world. And whatever barn you go to, you automatically have new friends, friends who love the same thing you do . . . HORSES!

And did I mention how cute the outfits are?

I'm sure a lot of you know how to ride (or even have horses). Please write and tell me about your riding, or send me pictures of your horse. If you don't ride . . . go try it, take a lesson or go on a trail ride. Just remember that horses are really big, and really stupid, so you have to be firm with them. (Oops, that's the old horseback-riding teacher in me coming out. . . . Just have fun!)

The girls are heading off to England next. I can't wait to see what happens there!

Write soon,
Mallory